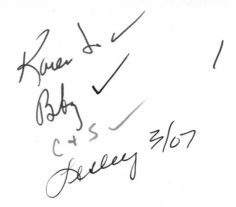

Twist of Fate

Jessica Casavant

Yellow Rose Books

Nederland, Texas

ISBN 1-932300-007-4

First Printing 2003

9 8 7 6 5 4 3 2 1

Cover design by Linda Callaghan

Published by:

Yellow Rose Books
PMB 210, 8691 9th Avenue
Port Arthur, Texas 77642-8025

Find us on the World Wide Web at
http://www.regalcrest.biz

Printed in the United States of America

Acknowledgments:

I would like to thank my tiny "cavalry" of friends, Ileana, Jane and Selena who have my gratitude for their support and their faithful reading of every story.

Day, who made editing painless and fun and never tired of teaching me about punctuation.

Linda (Calli) for creating a hundred covers and only crying once at my new ideas.

The entire Regal Crest team for their tireless efforts in making this publication possible.

Cathy for reading every version of every page.

For Cathy,
for everything.

Chapter
One

"Does the name Madison Williams ring a bell?"

At the name, Lauren's heart dropped. She fought to keep her face blank. "Should it?"

Keith McGraw studied her, searching for the truth on her face, in her eyes. It was second nature for him to pounce on any sign of weakness. As a reporter, he knew from years of chasing after the big story that he was on the verge of one. Instinct, or whatever you called it, had the hair on the back of his neck rising. He gave little thought to the fact that it might come at the expense of someone who had once been a friend. In his inside coat pocket he knew he was carrying dynamite, and felt no qualms about using it.

"We have reason to believe that she is a woman that you had an affair with a few years ago." He waited for her reaction.

Instinctively Lauren turned away. Her mind scrambled with the implication of Keith's discovery. She was overwhelmed by it: two years of silence shattered; her own emotions breaking loose. How could you ever prepare for a moment like this? It was like watching a bomb exploding in the distance, and all you could do was try and survive the aftermath of the explosion with as many body parts intact as possible.

"If you know all that, why come to me?" The question was foolish, a way of buying time.

Keith's tone was level. "You know why. We're asking you for comment."

She turned to look at him, and then anger overtook her—at the devastating consequence of his question, at this betrayal of their friendship. All those evenings they had shared once upon a time playing poker in the back of the press bus, destroyed by one innocent-sounding question.

"Give me a break. You're asking for help. It's the reporter's oldest trick: say whatever might have happened as if it's true, then hope your victim confirms it."

Keith watched her eyes. "This is hard for me," he said at last. "It's also my job. You should know, you've done this to people a hundred times. You'd do it to me if you had to."

She had put him on the defensive, Lauren saw. It gave her time to consider who could know about Madison. Snoopy neighbors were not enough. Where had the story come from? It wouldn't be Madison; she was certain of that.

"Were you having an affair?" he persisted.

Lauren's thoughts moved quickly. "Keith, I won't dignify this on or off the record. You show up and float some innuendo— planted months before the convention by God knows who— that could ruin lives, and you expect an answer? If you want anything from me, tell me what you think you've got and where it comes from."

As the heavy-set man crossed his arms, silent, Lauren felt a momentary buoying of confidence. Keith needed two credible sources, and there was no way he could have them.

Then he said, "Sit down, Lauren."

The words held a compassion that unnerved her more than what had come before. Slowly she crossed the room and sat. Keith took some papers from his pocket—two pages stapled together— and placed them in her hands. Lauren read the first words. Shock came first, then nausea. A film of tears kept her from reading more, sheer will the only thing that kept her from bolting.

"Leave. Please."

He shook his head, almost in regret. "You know I can't. Not yet."

Lauren turned from him and waited until she could read again. The notes were scattered, but for Lauren each line was devastating shorthand for all that she had been repressing for two tortured years. She saw herself as she was then, sobbing helplessly in the therapist's office, with no strength left for herself. All that she had wanted was for Madison to be with her.

Lauren stood, the papers clutched in her hand. "If this is true," she told him, "someone has violated my privacy in a terrible way. Shouldn't that bother you just a little?"

"Personally, yes. Professionally, it can't. This story's too important." He stepped closer to face her, and Lauren fought off the urge to step back. "This is news. It *is* true, isn't it?" His pale blue eyes fixed on her.

She could feel his excitement. It was palpable between them. They stared at each other, each unwilling to give in, to look away. Lauren made herself detach, think like a reporter. Someone might have seen Madison leaving her New York apartment, maybe even the house in the Cape, but that in and of itself proved nothing and could even be a mistake. No one knew who Madison was, so why would they remember her? *Newsbeat* was aggressive, but not unethical. They needed more than what they had. She went with her instincts. "No, it's not true. I hope that's not too upsetting."

He shook his head admiringly. She was cool; he gave her that. "Well...aside from the therapist's notes, we have records of long distance calls from you to her at all hours of the night. We have neighbors who saw her leaving your place in New York at all hours of the night." He paused. Did she really want him to go on?

"Let me understand this," Lauren said at last. "You've gotten notes from a psychologist—who has violated her legal obligation of confidentiality, *if* these papers are not a forgery. You've stolen my cell phone records. You've harassed my neighbors, telling anyone who might listen—though you can't know for certain—that I've had an affair. Why? Because my husband is running for office?"

Keith did not show that her words made him uneasy. "Do you deny starting an affair?"

Lauren fixed him with a cool, unblinking stare. "An affair? Yes, I deny it. If what you *do* have – phone calls and visits—is news, by all means, print away. You can try to rationalize this as news, just the way you have. But you also know that all the pressures to rationalize such tripe as noteworthy aren't really about reporting the news. It's about magazines like yours losing its audience to television and tabloids. Standards are so low these days, it's hard to find them even with a road map. We all know scandal sells more advertising, whether based on fact or fiction."

By now, little surprised her. Nothing made Lauren unhappier than to peer beneath the surface of someone's life at the anomalies, sad or sordid, which shadowed them. Lauren was too aware of her own secrets not to fear the consequences of exposing those of other people. She could see that in the most personal of moments were the simple truths. The true irony was that, as a journalist, it was her job to ferret out the lies hiding in the little truths; but at what cost?

Year after year, the press fed the public with sordid, private images on television. The fabric of it made everyone disregard decency, respect, and privacy. Where was the compassion, the averting of eyes at a tragedy? Was there anyone now in public office with a pristine background, a blank slate? How realistic was it to expect that none of the leaders would have skeletons in their closets? Who didn't have something to be ashamed of, some youthful indiscretions? Wasn't perfection an impossible standard to ask of someone, anyone? Wasn't a flawed leader who understood and faced up to his flaws more capable of leading with compassion than a leader who ignored his fallibility?

Lauren fought down her frustration and pain. She couldn't blame Keith for doing his job. She had been doing the same job for years. "That this story, if you print it, stands to benefit your career as surely as it will destroy three others is a moot point for you, isn't it?"

As Keith regarded her in continued silence, Lauren felt her anger drain. It was replaced by the knowledge of her own failings, her lies, the image of Madison.

In a quiet voice, Keith asked, "Are you telling me that it is true, but that in good conscience we shouldn't print it?"

For a moment, Lauren wanted to answer honestly, as one human being speaking to another. He was a good man; she knew that.   But this was about far more than her. "They're not your friends," her husband was fond of saying, warning her about the tightrope she was walking between being a senator's wife and a reporter.

"What I'm saying," Lauren answered simply, "is that it never happened. Your conscience is your own concern."

They stared at each other for a moment. "You're sure about this, Lauren?"

"Wouldn't you be?"   Lauren was the first to look away. "No more questions. You should leave now, Keith. It was good seeing you again." She turned her back to him, fighting off the urge to wrap her arms around herself protectively.

Keith sensed she was lying. He had watched her. She understood everything: the position she was in, what he was trying to do, what he needed from her. But it could not change the wounded look in her eyes, the delay in answering—however brief— as she struggled with how she felt. He grabbed the notes and turned to leave.

"Keith?" He paused at the door. "My husband is a good man, who is running for office because he believes that he can make a difference. If you are insisting that the public has a right to know, ask yourself this: who wins in the long run? Be careful that you are not being used as a pawn for someone trying to further his own political agenda. The timing of this is suspicious, don't you think?"

Keith had recovered his bearings. He shook his head. "Perhaps. But you should have thought of that before betraying him, Lauren. This is not over. It can't be. One day you might be our first lady, and that fact alone makes you part of the public's right to know. You are as much a part of the campaign story as your husband is. After the Clinton years, the American public is tired of anything that even smells of scandal when it comes to the White House, and your husband has made that point a big part of his campaign. You are both being touted as a breath of fresh air coming to Washington. How can this, then, not be part of the dialogue?" He didn't expect an answer. For a moment he felt sorry for her, but the moment passed. He was just doing his job, after all. "I'll be in touch." He shut the door softly.

Inside, Lauren leaned her face against the door. The only sound was that of her breathing. When the sickness came, she barely made it to the bathroom. Her body trembled as she vomited. Slowly she got up and lay across the bed, face buried in her pillow. What had happened with Madison would get out now. Even if *Newsbeat* never printed it, their reporters would continue to interrogate her neighbors, ask her friends if she had confided in them, spreading the rumors as they went. Soon the affair would be gossip at cocktail parties, then a story in the tabloids. The only question was whether to tell Matt now—before his campaign was affected, give him a chance to formulate a response now before it came out. She shivered as she imagined his reaction. How ironic that what she had tried so hard to avoid those scant years ago was now just around the corner. Two years of trying to pretend that she hadn't lived one of those once-in-a-lifetime moments and walked away from it had all come undone. *How did I get here?* She stared into the darkness.

Chapter
Two

Four years earlier

Madison Williams stood at the edge of the water, her bare feet sinking into the soft, white sand. The wet sand was like ice against the soles of her feet. The sky in front of her had sunk into the Atlantic Ocean that morning, swallowing her in steel gray.

The early June heat wave that had come to the East Coast so unexpectedly had disappeared overnight, replaced by unseasonably cold temperatures. She narrowed her eyes against the cool mist that was falling, her tears keeping company with the rain. She didn't feel the cold slice of it as the wind lifted and toyed with her loose dark hair. She was oblivious to the rain that had soaked her T-shirt and cotton pants, the wet material now clinging to her skin. The goose bumps on her bare arms went unnoticed as she stared unseeing into the gray.

The phone call had come shortly after two that morning. For such devastating news, the call had been brief. A life neatly wrapped up in thirty seconds. Samantha was dead, shot by a small-time drug dealer. Short and to the point, the words had delivered the message. Today the newspaper pages would have the story of another cop killed in a botched take-down. The outrage would quickly follow. But too soon the city would go back to living unaffected, and the officer's family and friends would be left alone to struggle with the fact that she was never coming home. Madison was one of those friends, left to bury someone not yet forty. And just like that, life turned on a dime. She wiped her tears and turned toward the house. She had a funeral to get ready for.

"I called Lauren Taylor last night," Jamie told Madison, who had showed up on her doorstep that morning. The tall, long-

legged blonde stood in her living room in her lacy bra and silk
boxers and pretended nonchalance as she started to iron her shirt.
Madison's eyebrows lifted at that statement.   Jamie had had a
mad crush on Lauren, her friend since college, for years. It had
become an inside joke between Jamie and Madison. Part of the
joke was that Lauren had no clue. She split her time between New
York, where she worked as a reporter, and Washington, where she
lived, and was often dropping by Boston to visit her friends with
little advance notice. Madison had never met her, and she had
always been curious about this woman her friends raved about.

"And?"

"And she's catching the next flight from Washington."

"Alex will be happy she is coming."

"Yeah. I know that she was hoping she could be here." There
was a pause as they both thought about the reason for the unexpected reunion. The grief was there, just under the surface. It was
a wound too new to examine, too fresh to absorb.

"How about you? Are you okay with her coming? From what
I remember hearing, the last time you got drunk and almost made
a fool of yourself," Madison told her, tongue in cheek.

Jamie made a face at that. " I admit, not one of my finest
moments. It's all under control. I mean, it was a long time ago."

"Uh-huh. Do you want me to go the airport with you?" Madison asked helpfully.

Jamie smiled. "No, that's okay. I'm a big girl. I'm sure I can
handle picking her up without tripping all over my tongue.
Though I haven't had sex in over three months..." She continued
to iron her shirt for a moment, then stopped. "No, it will be okay."
Her tone implied doubtful conviction as she resumed her ironing.

Madison watched the toned arms going through the motions.
Her mouth curved. "Mmm. You know, if I didn't know any better,
I would say that you're nervous about seeing Lauren again."

Jamie gave an unladylike snort. "Please..."

Madison straightened from her perch on the arm of the
couch. "Right, then." Again her lips twitched. "I have to go, I
promised Alex that I would get there early." Her dark gray eyes
gleamed as she looked at the semi-naked woman in front of her.
She turned to leave, then paused at the door. "See ya later. Oh,
and Jamie?"

Jamie's eyebrows disappeared into her blond bangs.

"I find that the process usually works better if you plug the iron in." With a soft laugh she was gone, the closing door muffling the frustrated curse.

Madison arrived early to help Alex with the final preparations for the funeral. Truth was, she was more than glad of a reason to stay busy. Samantha's death had completely side-swiped them all. No one ever expected to lose a friend who was still so young, though maybe there was a bit of naïveté in that thought. They had been lucky over the years in that their group of friends had escaped loss until now. She felt helpless to do anything to ease the grief. At least for a moment, she felt useful. She could also keep a close eye on Alex, who had been operating on autopilot since the death of her partner. There had been no tears, no hysterics, just quiet calm and firm resolve. It was unnerving to be around her, and her friends, Madison included, kept a close watch, expecting a breakdown at any moment.

Madison's eyes drifted to the front door, pulled there by the distant drone of traffic as it opened. She then forgot to breathe as she stared past Jamie to the woman who had followed her in. She was stunning, so much so that it almost hurt to look at her. Like staring into the sun too long. Long, dark blond hair was pulled back into a ponytail, leaving her face and all of its sharp angles breathtakingly in focus. Her eyes were an unusual shade of brown. *Almost closer to gold,* mused Madison, then her mind went blank as those eyes fixed on her then on Alex, who had entered the room from the kitchen.

"Lauren!" Alex hurried to her, and Lauren Taylor dropped her suit bag and enveloped Alex in a tight hug. For a moment, Madison almost felt jealous of her friend.

"Hey, kiddo."

"I'm so glad you are here."

Lauren held her tighter. "Me, too. I'm so sorry, Alex." For a moment tears came, but were quickly suppressed. There would be plenty of time for that.

Madison's attention turned to Jamie, who was smirking at her. For one brief, embarrassing moment, Madison had the uneasy suspicion that her mouth had been hanging open. She shifted when Jamie flopped down on the couch beside her, breaking the spell.

"Survived the drive, did you? Made an ass of yourself yet?"

Madison whispered to her.

Jamie snorted. "Shut up. I can see you drooling."

"Well, I'm not dead." Madison replied, then a look of horror crossed her face as she realized what she had just said. Jamie realized it at about the same time and they both burst out laughing, the laughter releasing some of the emotional overload they had been feeling.

Alex threw them a quick, puzzled look over Lauren's shoulder and half waved toward them. "Ignore my idiot friends over there." She released her hold and stepped back. "Wow, you get better looking every year. There ought to be a law."

"Or a pill," Jamie said with a grin.

At that comment, Lauren looked over at Jamie and made a face.

Jamie waved a hand toward Madison. "This is the other idiot friend, Madison, the doctor."

Lauren shot her a glance, the golden eyes drilling through her, looking at her and into her. The effect was immediate and powerful. Madison felt the jolt of it, and her mouth went suddenly dry.

Lauren stepped toward her, offering her hand with a smile. "Lauren Taylor. I've heard a lot about you."

"Madison Williams. Don't believe a word of it." As her fingers closed around the other woman's hand, she felt the touch of cool skin burn right through her. It felt like a shot of electricity passing through her fingertips. Puzzled, Madison took a cautious step back.

Lauren looked at her, something flickering across her face, then released her grip. For a moment as their eyes met once again, Lauren felt a shiver of recognition go through her, but the moment passed, and Lauren wondered if she had imagined it.

Madison sat straight backed on the wooden pew, the sweet, cloying smell of flowers overpowering. Flower arrangements were everywhere, filling the altar and both sides of the church. She would never again smell carnations without recalling this moment. Her eyes avoided the front where the gleaming mahogany casket rested, Samantha's police cap and badge sitting on a blue velvet cushion on top of it. On all sides, the rows were filled with uniformed officers from various police detachments from around the country. The loss of a cop was always felt deeply throughout the ranks, like the loss of a member of the family. The officers had rallied around in a tight circle, the death of one of their own another stark reminder of the very real danger they faced each day. Thousands more, she knew, were standing out on the street waiting to march in the funeral procession.

All around her she heard sounds of weeping and could feel everyone's sadness washing over her in waves as the chief of police gave the eulogy in a choked voice. His grief over losing another one of his officers was stamped in the deep creases of his face. Yet it was as if Madison were drifting above it, looking down at everyone. Intellectually, she knew she felt sadness and grief. But those emotions had quickly been buried deep within, covered by a detached numbness. It was the same feeling that enveloped her whenever she lost a patient she had come to care about. It didn't take a shrink to figure it all out.

This coping mechanism, developed after losing too many patients to incurable diseases, was now well ingrained. It was getting stronger every year. She had become adept at not letting herself feel loss. She glanced to her left at the pew in front of her, to Alex, who sat watching the service, face ravaged but eyes dry. As Madison's head turned back, her eyes met Lauren's tear-filled ones. There was an understanding in Lauren's look that unsettled Madison. It was as if Lauren knew what she was thinking. Without acknowledging it, she let her gaze drop down to her lap. She was surprised to see that her hands were clenched, and she felt the hard swallow from the grief in her throat. The lump wouldn't dislodge.

Following the noon service, the funeral concluded under suddenly threatening skies, with the sad, lonely sound of a bagpipe breaking the quiet. Madison stood apart from the group, staring up at the turbulent clouds. *It's as if the gods are angry*, she thought fancifully. The wind lifted and crossed the cemetery with a biting edge. She stood watching and absorbing it, unable to process the details of what was going on. Her eyes drifted to the mound of dirt piled on one side and she repressed a shiver, unable to accept that soon this pile would cover Samantha. She still felt numb, all feelings having drained from her the first moment she saw the casket.

Lauren swallowed the grief burning in her throat, her hand wiping at tears that continued to fall. She looked over at Madison, who was looking lost and alone despite the crowd. Then Madison's eyes lifted and latched on to hers, and Lauren's breath caught in her throat. There was a storm brewing in those eyes as the gray color shifted and darkened. *How could eyes like that be anything but lonely?* Lauren took a mental step back from thinking about it further. She dismissed the thought as the group quietly broke up and started back toward the parking lot in subdued clusters.

Lauren looked around for Jamie, who had been her ride, but could not find her. She glanced at Madison, who was walking a step behind, hands buried in her coat pockets, head down. "Can I get a ride with you? I seem to have lost Jamie."

"Sure. Come on."

In the car, as they pulled away, Madison glanced at her, trying to think of something to say. She felt tongue-tied, and was half amused, half irritated at the effect that this woman appeared to have on her.

"It was a beautiful service," Lauren finally said in the quiet of the car.

"Yeah." She downshifted as they neared an intersection.

"How long have you known Alex and Samantha?" Lauren asked, curious about this friend of a friend.

"Almost 10 years. You?"

"I went to high school with Alex, a lifetime ago it seems. I met Sam through Alex.   How did you meet them?"

Madison's face lightened as amusement entered her eyes. "About 10 years ago, I was pulled over by Samantha after a night of drowning my sorrows."

Lauren started to smile. "Really?"

Madison glanced at her and then backed to the road. "Really. I had just been dumped and was driving too fast, and Sam chased after me for about a mile until I finally pulled over." She grinned at the memory. "Man, she was something. Just out of police college, all strut and arrogance."

Lauren smiled at the image, delighted at the story. "Did you get a ticket?"

Madison glanced at her, her eyes shifting to a soft, dancing gray. "Nah. Got her phone number instead."

Lauren turned to look at her fully. "You went out with Sam?" She had never heard that story.

"Yeah, for about a minute. We went out for coffee the next

day, and immediately realized that we were meant to be lifelong friends. I never even got to first base." She shook her head as she pulled into the driveway. It did feel like it was a lifetime ago. Her eyes were suddenly haunted as she remembered that Sam was gone. "Funny how quickly life can change when you least expect it."

Their eyes met and a slow shiver went through Lauren. "Do you believe in fate?"

"Not really."

Lauren unhooked her seat belt. "I do." She said it softly. "I believe that everything happens for a reason. Though at times like these it's hard to figure out what those reasons are." Their eyes met briefly, and then she stepped out of the car and turned to the house. Madison watched her go, wondering why her pulse was racing.

Later, as everyone busied themselves with the drinks and tiny sandwiches that had been set up at the house, Madison found herself standing alone beside Lauren for a moment. She stood by the table, hands holding tightly to her glass as conversations flowed around her, a mixture of laughter and shared memories and quiet grief. She stood stock-still, swallowing heavily as she felt the walls fast closing in on her, and she looked around in panic. She was going to lose it. Her eyes met Lauren's quietly watchful ones, and she felt the need to say something, anything, to break her quiet contemplation.

"How long are you here for?"

Lauren sipped her coffee. "I'm here for another day, then I have to leave."

"You want to grab dinner somewhere?" The question was out of her mouth before Madison had a chance to think about it.

"Dinner?"

"Yeah, you know: eating, time when food is served. You do eat, right?"

Lauren's mouth curved. "Occasionally."

"Good. I promise you good food and my almost undivided attention."

Her smile was faint, but to Lauren it was like watching the sun come out from behind dark clouds. She had no idea how, but she was won over. "Okay."

Madison took her to a small café near Alex's house. Lauren had walked by it a few times, but never gone in. It was a small, cozy spot that hinted of intimate conversations. The light was a diffuse blue that added a soft tint to the white flowers on the center of each table. The tables themselves were round, with deep chairs and small sofas circling them. At the glossy wooden bar, glasses sparkled. There was a comfortable spacing between the tables so you didn't feel like you were sitting with strangers. Right at home in the café, she called out to the bar, "Darcy, a Shiraz please." She turned to Lauren. "Want anything to drink?"

"Same, please."

"Make that two." She grinned, delighted. "I was ready to dislike you if you said white wine."

There was an amused curve to Lauren's mouth. "There is no such thing as a good white wine," she responded solemnly.

"Exactly," Madison agreed, pleased. She watched Lauren look around with interest and smiled, suddenly feeling the sorrow of her day lift. She turned to watch Darcy, the owner of the café and one of her closest friends, make her way to the table with the order. As Darcy neared, she saw Lauren and did a double take, almost spilling the wine in the process.

Madison grinned at the image of the always cool and collected Darcy losing her composure over a woman. It rarely happened. Her eyes met Darcy's, and the look they exchanged was amused acknowledgment of Lauren's impact. Darcy blushed as Lauren turned to thank her.

"You're welcome," she mumbled, then fled, unable to cope.

Madison started to laugh. Lauren looked at her, puzzled. "What?"

The appealing part was that she had absolutely no idea of the effect she had on people. Madison smiled. "Nothing. I'm just suddenly really happy to be here. I have no idea why."

Lauren smiled back at her. "Me, too."

Their eyes held for a moment, then Madison broke the contact to glance at the menu. She knew it by heart, but she wanted, no, needed, an excuse to stop staring. Lauren would think her rude...or crazy.

Lauren seemed content with the silence and turned her attention to the menu. "What do you recommend?"

"I always have the Darcy Salad. Usually I'm eating here after a late shift, and the salad ends up being just the perfect meal. But pretty much everything here is good."

Lauren read the description on the menu. "Oh, avocado."

"Yeah. You don't like it?" It was Madison's favorite.

"'Like' is probably not the word I would use. It's a bit of an obsession with me." She leaned closer, her voice dropping to a quiet whisper. "Sometimes I'll peel an avocado and sprinkle some pepper on it, and sit out on my patio munching away as I plan my garden. Everyone think it's revolting. I don't care." Her grin was wide. "It's heaven." She sat back.

Madison looked at her blankly. Surely this had to be fate. She returned the smile, amused at her thoughts, then went to the bar to order their salads, knowing that Darcy was trying to give them some privacy.

"So, tell me about yourself." Lauren asked as she returned to the table.

"What? Oh, I won't bore you with the gory details." Madison tried to dismiss the inquiry.

"Do you always have a hard time talking about yourself?"

"Yes. I mean no." Her grin was wry.

Something in the way Lauren looked at her, focused on her, had Madison desperately wanting to spill it all out—talk about her frustration, her fear, the loneliness she felt. That terrible loneliness of being the doctor with the bad news was starting to get to her after all these years. She was getting too good at hiding her thoughts, at shutting down and detaching from her feelings. She was afraid she was becoming cold and unfeeling. Her reaction to Samantha's death had brought it all into focus. She sighed.

"I guess I am getting tired of not winning the fights as a doctor and as a friend. There are two possible outcomes in oncology, which is my specialty. One is we never find out what is wrong and it becomes a mystery, filled with symptoms and endless tests and frustration because you can't help the patient in any way. The other outcome is death. There is no beating it. Sometimes I get lucky, and I can delay it a bit, but even that becomes bittersweet." How many times had she looked across at the patient and their loved ones and seen the fear and the hope in their eyes? "Make me better. Help me," they all seemed to say. She took a long sip and placed her glass back down on the table. "I've sat at a patient's bedside and held their hands for hours, sometimes falling asleep with them. I used to see it as a privilege to be there, even when they were dying; to help a family rather than only seeing the pain and the hurt. It can be wearing after a while. I'm at a point where I almost feel like I've stopped feeling. Even now, with Sam's death, I haven't been able to truly cry. The control that I seem to have over my feelings scares me."

Lauren did not fill the silence with platitudes; she simply listened, her face reflecting her empathy. "It's an awesome responsibility, being asked to play God sometimes."

They exchanged glances and Madison shook her head. "Sorry. I didn't mean to get all dark and gloomy. I just..." She stopped when Lauren took her hand. Lauren didn't say anything, but her thumb gently rubbed against one of her knuckles. The motion seemed so natural, so perfectly right, that Madison was overwhelmed with the urge to cry. How could this woman she didn't even know make her want to feel so much after such a short time? The thought was unsettling. "Like recognizes like," she had heard someone say. Maybe this was all it was. Then Lauren's eyes met hers, and Madison suddenly had a flash of insight that this could be more. She swallowed down her panic and smiled at Lauren.

Lauren returned the smile. There was such sweetness to her smile that Madison could only stare at her, amazed at the sheer beauty in front of her.

"So, I have to ask. Madison? It's an unusual name. Beautiful, but unusual."

Madison grinned. "The rumor is that I was conceived on Madison Avenue in New York City. I've always been afraid to ask where. I always thought it would be a bit creepy to find out it was in the elevator at Bloomingdale's, or some such thing. I could never shop there again." She sipped her wine. "Knowing my mother, I wouldn't put it past her, though."

"Are you close?"

"No. We exchange cards at Christmas and birthdays, if we think of it. That's really the extent of our communication." Something in her eyes told Lauren that the subject was sensitive, and she let it go. Madison didn't want to spoil her evening by thinking or talking about her mother, so she changed the subject.

"How about you? Are you close to your family?"

"No not really. I am the eighth of nine, and somewhere along the way my family tended to forget about the younger kids."

"Nine kids? Good Lord."

Lauren shrugged. "Irish and Catholic."

There was pain there, Madison sensed. "Was it hard living your life?"

It was an unusual question, and Lauren took the time to think about it. "I've always felt that I was a visitor in my own life, like I wasn't quite a full member of this large clan. Not that I wasn't wanted; more like I didn't matter. There were too many of us, I guess. My parents were too much into themselves, too busy with each other to remember that each child might require something more."

She toyed with her glass, amazed at how easy talking suddenly seemed to be. "The only thing that I truly wanted was to walk into a room and see my parents' faces light up, just to show how delighted they were that I came along. That acknowledgment would have made the difference." She smiled ruefully. "How needy is that?"

Madison looked at her quietly. "Not needy, just real. There is nothing wrong with wanting affirmation that you matter."

She was looking at Lauren, really looking at her, and it was as if the air stilled...or something. A certain kind of quiet descended between them.

The blonde's throat grew tight as Madison continued to gaze at her. Lauren cleared her throat and looked away. "Now my mother just leaves me messages on my machine. Today, for example, I got five. Five! She wants her youngest daughter—that would be me—to think about children again. She wants more grandchildren before she's too old to bounce a baby on her frail old knee. I get this every time one of her friends has another grandchild. She hasn't accepted the fact that I can't have children. After all of these years, she still somehow thinks it's all a cruel joke I perpetuate just to distress her."

Madison was intrigued by the story. "So why can't you have children?"

"Hmm? Oh, there's something wrong with my eggs. They're the wrong size. Matt and I have tried to conceive over the years, but finally gave up."

"Matt?"

Lauren briefly hesitated. "My husband."

Madison's eyes glanced down to Lauren's ringless hand, and absorbed the sudden, acute disappointment she felt. *Figures.* She should have paid more attention to Jamie's babbling. She often tuned out gossip, and she was sure that the topic of Lauren being married would have come up. She tried to remember.

Lauren saw the disappointment and was saddened by it. She

stared past Madison. "I wanted to adopt, but Matt is against the idea."

Madison strengthened. "I'm sorry. I didn't mean to bring up anything painful for you."

Lauren shook her head. "You didn't. I've had plenty of time to get used to it." Unable to stop herself, she touched Madison's hand again. She was used to the guilt, the feelings of failure that crept through her whenever Matt brought it up—casually, almost as a joke. Except it wasn't funny, and she knew that deep inside Matt blamed her for not being able to produce the child that would make them the perfect golden couple marching in lock-step to the White House. She knew that Clarence, Matt's campaign manager and his closest aide, had even done polls on the subject of children vs. no children years before to gauge their chances either way. *Imagine planning our personal life around polls.* She still couldn't get used to the idea of living like that: all decisions based on percentages and returns.

She shook herself. There was no sense reliving those thoughts. What was done was done. She glanced at Madison, who was looking around the restaurant. *What is she thinking?* Lauren wondered, suddenly filled with an ache so acute that it took her breath away for a moment. She wanted Madison's arms around her. She wanted to bury her head against that sturdy shoulder and feel that quiet strength against her. And was amazed at those feelings. *Where did that come from?*

Lost in her own thoughts, Madison looked down at their still-joined hands and was surprised to see they were still holding hands. Her eyes lifted and met Lauren's waiting look, and something shifted deep inside of her. The golden eyes looking back at her darkened in acknowledgment of the feelings suddenly weighing on them, then she removed her hand. Trembling, Madison grabbed her wine and took a long swallow, trying to moisten her suddenly dry throat. Lauren looked away, unnerved by what she was feeling. Thankfully, the arrival of their meal provided a distraction.

"So, what do you do?" the dark-haired woman asked Lauren between mouthfuls.

"I'm a journalist for *News Hour.*"

"*News Hour?*"

She smiled ruefully at the blank look on Madison's face. "You know, if I had issues with my ego, your reaction would be devastating."

Madison grinned. "Sorry, I don't really watch television. It's television, right?"

"Uh-huh...it is a newsmagazine, like *60 Minutes,*" Lauren clarified dryly. "I used to cover the White House as one of their correspondents. That is, until a few months ago, when my husband decided he might want to be president. To avoid any appearance of bias in my reporting, I now do puff pieces out of our studio in New York." It still rankled that she had had to change her career, her focus, all because Matt was toying with the idea of going beyond the Senate. He had not even given it a second thought. It was expected of her, and that was that.

"President? Who is your husband?"

"Matthew Taylor."

"Our senator?" Madison felt the disappointment intensify. She vaguely remembered seeing the young senator from their state at some hospital function or another, but never Lauren. She definitely would have remembered. As far as the senator was concerned, she had never voted for him. He was too polished for her tastes. She now thought of that with irony.

"Even though the campaign is two years away, he has started raising funds, being pursued, doing the pursuing. It's a bit like selling yourself to the highest bidder. It's a strange life." For Lauren, who always took pride in her work, the last years had not been good years. Covering Capitol Hill, she saw it all: petty men taking small chances for selfish reasons, trying to manipulate just enough of a cynical public to keep themselves in office. The depressing result for journalists was that they, too, had become less important, reduced to covering politics as if it were a horse race. Their thoughtful pieces were demoted from the front page to a place well behind the coverage of the latest murder trial. And just as damaging for all concerned was the competition to report on personal scandal, warmed to a white heat by the tabloids, which seemed to have diminished both the standards of reporting and the standing of politicians in general. She still didn't understand Matt's desire to get involved in the thick of the madness.

Madison heard something in the undertones. She studied the woman across from her. "How do you feel about becoming first lady?"

"Like I want to run screaming in the opposite direction." She sighed. "I don't want to be a wife that has to give up my life, friends, and career to be an afterthought in someone else's."

In effect, she knew, she already was. She was now just another cog in the machine carrying them all to the White House. She toyed with the stem of her glass, fighting the urge to touch her dinner companion again. The pause between them held undercurrents of a physical awareness of each other that they both tried to ignore.

"So, how did you decide to become a journalist?"

Lauren's smile was dry. "You say it like it's a revolting profession."

Madison started to laugh. "Did I? Sorry." Her brow lifted as she waited for an answer.

Sitting back, Lauren took in the light and shadow of the restaurant, felt the glow of the wine. "*How I Became a Journalist,* by Lauren Taylor. I became a journalist because..."

"Yes?"

"Do you want to hear this or not?" she asked, thoroughly enjoying herself.

"Sorry." The exchanged grins.

"Okay, I became a journalist because when I was young, I liked to read—everything, even the newspaper. Naturally that meant I was the 'smart one.' I was attending an all-girls Catholic school, and so with only girls in class, I developed a very rich fantasy life, with me at the center. The school—run by nuns, by the way—encouraged me to sublimate through writing." She smiled. "In between writing bad short stories and imagining I was Ernest Hemingway, I became the star of the school newspaper. In the end, reality beat out fantasy."

"Are you sure?" Madison said lightly. "Or have you just found a way to combine them?"

"Oh, I'm sure." Lauren shook her head. "Writing fiction usually doesn't pay. When you've got no money, you discover things like that. Even in high school. It doesn't stop me from wishing I could do more with my writing, but a girl has to pay her bills, too."

"Do you like it?"

"What?"

"Digging into peoples' lives."

Lauren looked at her for a beat, looking for the sarcasm. There was only quiet interest. She hesitated, wondering where the need for total honesty had come from. "Sometimes I don't. Sometimes I keep feeling that I should do something else with my life besides 'digging into peoples' lives,' as you say. I'm certainly not out there saving lives..."

Madison frowned at that. "I wasn't implying that what you do is not worthy..."

"I know; I was. I admire people like you, Madison. People that are giving something back to humanity. Let's just say that I have been doing a lot of soul searching on a lot of topics lately. You just touched a nerve because I have been thinking about this very seriously. How about you? How did you become a doctor?"

Madison suddenly smiled, her eyes dancing. "I don't want to destroy your illusions."

Intrigued, Lauren smiled back. "You can't get away with that statement without explaining."

Madison's fingers tapped lightly on the table. "I had a mad crush on my best friend in high school. Tina Rather was her name." She closed her eyes as she spoke the name. "She was something. She had the biggest..." She opened her eyes and answered Lauren's amused expression with a grin. "*Anyways,* she decided she wanted to become a doctor, so of course I decided that I wanted to be the same. We both applied to the university and registered for the same courses. Truth is, I chose my career path because she kept hugging me," she said with a shake of her head.

She lifted her eyes to Lauren, who burst out laughing. "You're kidding, right?"

"Nope." She smiled, enjoying Lauren's laughter.

"Whatever happened to this Tina?"

"Well...it appears that what Tina really wanted was not to *be* a doctor, but to marry one. So she did, in our first year." She sipped her wine. "I got my revenge, though; she married a bald podiatrist."

They shared a smile. As their eyes met, Madison felt the heat of her attraction collide with her common sense. With a quick glance at her watch, she rose with a strained smile. "I need to go. I have some early rounds in the morning." She was running away. She knew it, but could not stop herself from jumping up from the table as if her life depended on it.

"Please stay a bit longer." Lauren didn't know why she was pleading for a virtual stranger to stay, but she did not want the evening to end, did not want to see this woman disappear.

"I'm sorry, I can't." Madison was perceptive enough to know that Lauren was not totally immune to the feelings dancing all around them. It was too tempting to stay, and too dangerous.

"Thanks for the dinner and the conversation," Lauren responded stiffly, rising as Madison threw some money on the table.

"Lauren, I just…"

Lauren didn't pretend she didn't understand. Her look was steady, and something lurked in the depths of her eyes. "I know. Let's leave it at that."

Chapter
Three

"How hard is it to get someone to pee in a cup?" Madison felt the unmistakable beginnings of a headache creeping over her forehead as she stood talking on the phone.

"For crying out loud, Peg, you don't have to hold the cup for him. Just give it to him." She slammed the receiver down. *God, I miss Nancy,* she thought of her long-suffering nurse who was finally taking a well-deserved holiday. *I'm going to give her a raise and forbid her to ever take another day off again,* she thought half-seriously.

"What?" she barked out in response to the knock on the door.

"Is that the tone you use for your bedside manner?" A faint flicker that could have been amusement crossed Lauren's face as she peeked in. "Hello."

"Well, hello back." It had been a couple of months since the funeral, and Madison was ruefully aware that she was probably too delighted to see the newswoman standing so unexpectedly in her office.

Lauren smiled, then looked around the untidy office with interest.

"I'm surprised to see you again," Madison commented.

Lauren turned to her. "Are you?" They stared at each other, Lauren's look faintly curious.

Madison felt the hair at the back of her neck rise and couldn't answer. She shifted, breaking the spell.

Lauren smiled. After several fruitless calls and unreturned messages, she had given up in her attempts to get in touch directly with the doctor. "You didn't get my messages? I made an appointment for a consultation." She sighed when Madison shook her head. "I wanted to speak to you about..." Her voice trailed away as the phone started to ring and Madison grabbed it. Lauren frowned at the interruption. *Well, that was rude. Why is it so hard to get her to pay attention for one minute?*

But Madison had answered the phone more out of self-preservation. She knew better than to expect the temporary nurse to answer it. She had found out after a painful week of garbled messages that answering telephones seemed out of the temp's realm of expertise. Thank God Nancy was due back in a few days.

"Yeah?" For a moment Madison thought she had heard wrong, and she frowned against the pounding in her head. "What do you mean, they lost Kim's results? Where was it last?"

Lauren watched Madison close her eyes and deliberately push a breath through her body. Her left hand absently rubbed her temple. She opened her eyes and watched Lauren watching her, the moment strangely intimate. Lauren was the first to look away.

"Has this hospital been taken over by fools lately? I'm amazed you can find the phone over there! Well, I don't care what you have to do. Tear the place apart if you have to, but find me that damn biopsy." She slammed the telephone down and glanced at Lauren. "Sorry, what were you saying?"

"I wanted to talk to you about a possible patient." She sighed at the blank look on Madison's face. "Haven't you seen the file? Or gotten any of my messages?"

"Messages?" Madison brushed by her to open the door. "Peg? Any messages?"

"No, Doctor."

Madison turned and watched the flicker of frustration cross Lauren's face. "Temporary nurse filling in," she tried to explain.

The golden eyes were cool. "Obviously I have come at a bad time. Excuse me."

"Lauren?"

The quiet voice stopped Lauren as she turned to leave.

"I'm having a particularly bad day, wrapped around a particularly bad week. In order for me to continue having it without murdering anyone, I have to start my rounds. Can we talk about this later?"

Lauren caught the hint of exhaustion in the smoky eyes, the tension around the well-defined mouth.

"Will you call me, then? I'm having a hard time drumming up any enthusiasm for me calling you at the moment." The smile took most of the sting out of her words.

Madison looked up at her, pleased by the wit. "I'll go you one better. Let me buy you dinner tonight after I'm done. I'll search for the file, and we can go over it then."

Lauren had never seen eyes that smiled in quite that way before. She felt a flutter in her stomach and wisely chose to ignore it.

The dinner was not what they had initially planned, as an emergency kept Madison at the hospital late, and they ended up meeting down in the hospital cafeteria, gulping down lukewarm soup and very old coffee. Lauren didn't mind the wait, didn't even mind the location of their meeting, though she was not overly fond of hospitals. She had nothing pressing to do.

She looked around the cafeteria and wondered briefly why all hospitals looked the same: the same drab colors, the same hard plastic furniture, the same smell. It was the smell that got to her. No matter how strong the disinfectant, it was never strong enough to mask the smell of illness and decay. She turned her attention to Madison, who still managed after a long day to look incredible in her white lab coat, a forgotten stethoscope around her neck. *Incredible?* She ignored the tiny voice that warned her about these unexpected thoughts.

"So, who is this patient you want to talk to me about?"

"His name is Carlos. He came to my husband's office looking for help."

Ah yes, the husband, thought Madison grumpily. "How did you get him?" Her voice was a bit sharper than intended.

Lauren studied her, hearing the undertones but unsure of what they meant. "A lot of people show up at their senator's office looking for help. I have an arrangement with Matt's assistant. When she thinks I can help, she calls."

Madison couldn't think of anything to say to that, so she grabbed the file lying on the table beside her.

Lauren took a sip of coffee as the doctor flipped it open. Madison frowned as she read quickly through the chart and the various notes scattered across the pages. The boy was only five years old, with a variety of symptoms that pointed at everything and nothing. It always broke her heart when children became sick. She didn't know what was more difficult to deal with: the sick child, or the parent. Children who were sick were often braver than the parents who, too often, would collapse under the fear and strain.

"Reds are low. Platelets high. Night sweats, weight loss. Bone pains." She looked up at Lauren.

"What's your gut feeling?" Lauren asked, watching her eyes.

Madison pushed the file away. "Autoimmune disorder, maybe leukemia. Next step would be a bone marrow test. The blood work is not really conclusive. It doesn't give me much to work with, except to show that there is an issue. If you want, I can try to fit him in the next week or so."

"Yeah." Lauren took a breath and looked suddenly shy. "There's a bit of a catch."

Madison dark brow lifted.

"He has no money. No insurance."

"I'm a doctor, not a charity." Madison said, testing Lauren's reaction.

Lauren's look was level. She had expected as much and was willing to barter. "I'll give you my home on the Cape."

"To keep?"

"What? Oh, no. I meant for a summer break or something."

Madison started to laugh at the panic on Lauren's face.

Lauren smiled, getting the joke. "It would mean a lot to me if you could see him." Lauren fixed her golden eyes on the dark-haired woman, and she was lost.

"I'll do it, but just so you know that I'm not a total pushover, I might take you up on the offer of a getaway. One of these days, I am going to take some time off."

Lauren smiled and gently placed her hand over Madison's. "Thanks."

Madison's pager was loud in the sudden stillness. She made a face. "Sorry, I've got to go."

"Is there coffee?"

"No."

"Why not?"

The diminutive nurse peered over her glasses at Madison. "How many years have I worked for you?"

Madison marched grumpily into her office. "Too many."

"How many times have I made coffee?"

Madison came back into the outer office as she pulled her white lab coat on over her cream pants and brown T-shirt. "Would it hurt if just once you made the bloody coffee? Like maybe on my birthday?"

Nancy, a petite live wire with a no-nonsense attitude, grabbed her notepad. "It's not your birthday. And we've talked about this. I don't do coffee."

"Fine. I'll make the damn stuff myself." Madison stalked to the little kitchen in the back of the office, only to discover there were no coffee filters left. She banged the cupboard doors shut. "Dammit, Nancy, where are the filters?"

Nancy appeared beside her. "Should I put filters on your to do list?"

Madison stared at her exasperated. "You know, one of these days, I'm going to find myself someone who makes coffee."

Unperturbed, Nancy went back to pulling patients' files from the file cabinet. "Okay. You might want to look for one who answers phones, too. That seems to be a dying art."

Madison stared at her for a moment, looking for the sarcasm she was sure was there. "I'm going down to the coffee shop." At the door, Madison turned. "Oh, by the way, you are never allowed to take holidays again." She slammed out.

Nancy stared at the door, amused. "I've missed you, too."

She knew she should avoid drinking coffee; she was already feeling edgy, with the tension rumbling below the surface almost as if it had infiltrated her bloodstream. She hadn't slept again, and was loath to examine the reasons why. As she got to the coffee shop downstairs, she saw the reason for her sleeplessness walk in. This was the third time they had run into each other, and she wasn't sure if she should be as happy as she felt. It worried her. There was nothing more depressing than having a crush on a straight woman. Actually, there was—when it was on a straight, *married* one.

Lauren saw her from across the room and smiled.

Madison crossed to her. "Hello."

"Hello back."

"Want a coffee?" Madison asked automatically.

"No, thanks. I never touch the stuff, remember? Chai tea. That's my weakness. How are you?"

Madison found herself answering honestly. "Tired. I haven't really been sleeping lately."

"Me neither." They avoided looking at each other as they paid the cashier.

"Do I dare ask if it's safe to try and make an appointment for Carlos this week?"

Madison grinned. "Yeah. Nancy is back. Life is bound to get back to normal again." *At least work-wise*, she thought. "Call Nancy, she'll find you a spot."

Lauren looked at her, then away. "There's a small catch."

"Another one?"

Lauren grinned. "I will have to come with him. You see, his family only speaks a little English."

Madison's mouth twitched. "How little?"

"Hello and thank you. They're refugees from Cuba."

Madison stared at her and Lauren tried not to laugh out loud at the look on her face. "Well, this should prove interesting. I haven't used Spanish since high school. And even then it was rudimentary at best. "

"I'll be there to translate."

"I hope your vocabulary goes beyond 'another margarita, senorita.'"

"Barely. But it's a start."

Madison was staring at her notes without having any of the words register. She looked up at the knock. Nancy walked in, looking flustered. It was such an unusual occurrence for the usually unflappable nurse that Madison stared at her in confusion.

"Madison, there's a strange woman with a little boy in the waiting room. All they can say is Doctor-Doctor. I can't understand the rest."

"I'm assuming that that's Carlos. Isn't Lauren with them?"

"No."

"Well, show them in."

Madison stood up as the door opened, and stared at the short, wrinkled older woman who walked in, pulling a young boy by the hand. The brown face was creased into hundreds of lines that mapped into a lifetime. The dark eyes that regarded her glowed with strong energy.

"Hi. I'm Dr. Williams," she said slowly.

The old woman nodded her head several times and launched into rapid-fire Spanish.

Madison raised her hand. "Wait. Wait. I mean, slow down."
Neither one understood the other, but that didn't stop them from
trying to make sense of the broken conversation. *This is going to
be great,* she thought, trying to remember who on staff spoke
Spanish. Before she could summon help, the door swung open and
Lauren burst in.

"Sorry."

Madison had never been happier to see anyone.

"How's it going?"

"Well, we have already done the hello and thank you part. I
was about to order a tequila..."

Lauren started to laugh, then she knelt down by Carlos, who
was half buried behind the old woman's ample skirt. Madison
watched as Lauren coaxed him from behind the woman, all the
while talking softly to him in Spanish. She heard her name mentioned, and guessed that Lauren was telling him who she was.

She watched Lauren talk him into sitting on the examining
table, and felt a tug of envy when Lauren's hand caressed his face,
bringing a tiny smile to his brown face. Lauren turned to her with
a smile and motioned her closer.

"He's all yours." She stepped aside.

Madison looked at her, surprised, as Lauren appeared to be
getting ready to leave. She whispered a panicked aside, "Don't you
go anywhere."

Lauren grinned. "You're very cute when you're flustered."

Madison made a face, the exchange watched by the old
woman. She smiled at Lauren and said something in Spanish.
Lauren looked startled at what was said and shook her head,
unable to stop herself from blushing. The woman repeated it, a
knowing look in her dark eyes.

Madison frowned. "What is she saying?" *Damn, I wish I
understood Spanish.*

Lauren cleared her throat. "Nothing important." She couldn't
possibly tell her friend that the old lady had asked if they were
together. She didn't know why she felt so flustered by the thought.
She dismissed the topic by turning her attention to the boy.

Madison stared at her, then glanced at the old woman. The
woman nodded her head at her as if in agreement. Madison
wanted to ask again, but Carlos looked frozen, patiently waiting
on the table, dwarfed by all of the equipment. She pulled a tiny
giggle from him as she put on a Mickey Mouse hat she saved for

the kids.

In a mixture of halting Spanish and broken English they managed to get through the examination, the boy laughing as she mangled his language. His nose became his foot, his chest a finger. His high giggle was a delight, and brought a smile to all three women. All through the examination she was aware of Lauren's presence in the room, and part of her was tuned to her every smile, her every move. She arranged for a follow-up appointment for the bone marrow test, and saw them out.

After escorting them to the elevator, Lauren returned. She stood inside the open door and watched an unsuspecting Madison for a moment as she sat at her desk writing in Carlos' file, a look of absorbed concentration on her face. Forgotten was the Mickey Mouse hat still sitting on her head. *God, she is beautiful,* Lauren thought with a pang. As if sensing her, Madison abruptly lifted her head and looked her way.

"Hey, thanks for doing this." Lauren stepped into the room.

Madison stood up and walked around her desk to lean against the opposite corner. "He's adorable."

"Yeah. I'm always tempted to kidnap him and take him home with me," Lauren added with a smile. She continued to smile at her friend.

"What?" Madison asked, puzzled.

Lauren reached out and took off the mouse ears, her fingers lingering for a moment in the soft, dark strands of hair. With a grin, she handed her the hat. "Do you do other character impressions beside Mickey?"

Madison grinned. "Yeah, you should see my Pooh."

"I'm a Tigger woman, myself." It had been a long time since she had felt like playing, but being this close to Madison made her feel silly.

Their eyes met for a moment; both were intrigued, yet unsure of the next step.

Madison shifted, trying to avoid staring at Lauren's mouth too long. *But damn, it's a hell of a mouth...* "I hear that your husband will be the keynote speaker at the hospital fundraiser next week. Will you be there?" She kept her tone carefully neutral.

Clamping down on her feelings, Lauren took a step back. "Probably. Just one more rubber chicken dinner with overcooked string beans," she added, a hint of sarcasm in her tone. She looked at Madison hopefully. "Will you?"

"I wasn't planning on going. I hate those things..."

"Oh." Lauren hid her disappointment, but not quickly enough.

Madison hesitated. "I probably will this time, though. I'm the senior resident, so it's good for the department when I show up to charm money out of the locals." *Oh yeah, I'm in trouble.*

Lauren's smile was wide. "Then maybe I'll see you next week." She left, and her departure seemed to suck the energy out of the room. Madison stood staring at the door, overcome with sadness.

Nancy, who had come in, looked at her with concern. "Are you okay?"

"I think I'm falling in love, and I don't have any idea what to do about it," Madison answered, feeling completely lost.

"Are you wearing that?"

"That was the plan," Lauren answered as she adjusted the thin strap of her slim black dress. It fit her like glove, subtly accentuating the soft curves of her hips. The color complemented the golden hue of her skin, and brought out the golden highlights in her eyes and her hair. Glancing at Matt in the mirror, she caught his grimace. "Is there something wrong with it?" she asked, her tone level.

"No." He adjusted his tie, then turned to leave. At the door, he turned. "It's just that it's an important night for us, for the party. A lot of people with thick wallets will be attending this thing. It's important to get their support early." He shrugged.

Lauren swallowed the immediate retort that sprang to mind. He was talking to her as if she were an idiot. She was too fed up and exhausted by the charade they lived to try and put up even a token resistance. "Is there something else you want me to wear?"

"The blue one is nice." Without another word, he left the room.

She turned to her closet to pick out the dress. *The blue one makes me look like a sixty-year-old matron,* she thought. She quickly changed, and left the room without so much as a backward glance at the mirror. As they left for the dinner, he never even acknowledged that she had changed. It was expected, and that was that.

Madison looked around with amusement at the dressed-up crowd, the movers and shakers and pretenders of the city. The air was thick with phoniness and cloying chat. She had spent the better part of an hour with a fixed smile on her face, repeating the same inane patter. "How are you? It's *so* good to see you." She listened to the various conversations, feigning interest. "Really, who cares that your interior designer chose the wrong color of blue for the guesthouse?" she wanted to say. Instead, she made the appropriate sounds of distress. And through it all, a part of her knew where Lauren was at all times, could see her from a corner of her eye going through the room, a tall good-looking blonde at her side. Madison had recognized Matt from newspaper articles. Hadn't he made it into the *Hunks on the Hill* calendar once? She tried to remember. Did it really matter? Seeing Lauren with Matt brought everything into sharp focus.

She had seen Lauren on and off over the previous several days as they worked through the battery of tests for Carlos. Her attraction had increased each time they were together, and she knew she was on the verge of tumbling. Part of her had wanted to come to the fundraiser to finally meet him, hoping that seeing them as a couple would knock some sense into her. But now, Madison found it increasingly harder to watch Lauren with Matt. She felt her heart ache for what couldn't be and, feeling blue, she stepped out onto the balcony overlooking the private beach.

From across the room, Lauren watched her go, then turned to Matt to excuse herself.

Matt absently waved her away, turning back to the aging senator from New York. As the minority leader, the politician was a strong ally to have on his side; his word carried a lot of weight in the party. The night before, Clarence had reminded Matt that if he could get the senator's endorsement, he could lock in New York and another half-dozen states.

The veteran senator knew what the game was and looked at Matt shrewdly. "So, you've got the virus, do you? You looked around and decided you were better than anyone in sight?"

He had been in the Senate for over 30 years, and minority leader for the last eight. He liked young Matt and especially his lovely wife, but then again, women and alcohol had always been his two weaknesses. "That's only the first step. The easiest and the most deluded. Later you find out that the demands of a presidential campaign are much greater then you imagined, that the fishbowl you've entered is far more degrading, that the sheer enormity of what it takes to run for president—let alone the chance that you might win—threatens to overwhelm you."

Matt knew the advantages of silence. The old man was clearly not done. He waited, letting the senator call the shots.

The senator was warming up to his task, his fleshy face reddening. "It's not just begging for money from people you loathe and trying to look happy doing it. It's things like the afternoon I wasted in New Hampshire hunting for a fucking ceramic frog because a woman I needed for a delegate in Idaho collected them, and she was torn between our guy and two others who were leading in the polls." His eyes followed Lauren's progress across the room. "Will your wife be making a permanent move to Washington soon?"

This was a probe, Matt knew he was being examined, his weaknesses assessed. "No, not soon."

"Oh, she must. A serious run at the White House demands a total commitment. The public loves their white picket fences. They don't really care what really goes on behind the fences, they just require the illusion." He laughed at his jibe.

Matt knew there was a message in there somewhere. He nodded, a part of him almost annoyed at the important position that Lauren had in his campaign. *He* would be the candidate, not her. Yet he was pragmatic enough to know the assets a beautiful wife could bring to the mix. She hated campaigning, but he was confident she would be there when asked. He would make sure of that.

Madison leaned against the railing, ready to have a talk with herself. What good would it do to carry a torch for a married woman? There was no future in it...except heartache. What hurt the most was that it was the first time in her life that she had felt such an immediate connection to anyone. She sighed, looking up sadly at the stars. Which is how Lauren found her when she followed her out.

Without turning around, Madison knew Lauren had joined her. *Strange how the air seems to change,* she thought, *whenever she is near.*

Lauren leaned against the rail next to Madison and handed her a glass of champagne. They each took a sip, watching the inky surf attack then retreat from the sandy shore. Under the glow of the almost full moon, the shapes below took on an eerie blue light. The sound of the waves was strangely soothing in the moonlit night. After the heat of the crowded party, the cool breeze was refreshing.

"Enjoying the party?"

Madison shrugged. "I'm not much for these types of parties. I'm not very good with them. Especially when all everyone talks about is how so and so had their face or nose done, and doesn't it look awful? It's all so boring, and I usually end up insulting a doyenne of society."

Intrigued, Lauren glanced at the pure profile beside her, at the strong jaw where a muscle was now twitching. There was so much she wanted to know about this woman and her life: how she became who she was, her fears, her loves.

She had sensed their connection right from the first. Life had a strange way of creating events to wake people up from their self-induced comas, she believed. Timing was everything. At this, the most restless point in her life, she had met a woman she sensed could change everything. "When did you, you know, start batting for the other team?"

If Madison was surprised at the question, she didn't show it. She took her time answering as she sipped her drink. "I guess I've always batted for the other team. I mean, there were a few men now and then when I was younger, but honestly...nothing ever really compared."

"Compared to what?"

"To being with a woman. I love everything about making love to a woman: the softness of their skin, their mouths, the warmth of their bodies. There's nothing like it in the world, at least nothing that can compare." She swung her head around to glance at Lauren. "How about you? Have you ever been with a woman?"

Lauren felt the heat of the words dance over her skin. Lauren looked away to the water and sighed. "Almost. Once."

Madison watched her, intrigued. "Tell me about it." She was starved for every bit of information about her companion.

Lauren sipped her champagne, trying to find the words for her confusion, her search for the truth. She let the bubbles dance on her tongue for a beat. "I've been married for eleven years," she started cautiously.

"That's a long time," Madison said quietly.

"I guess." She looked back out to the water, trying to remember the girl of so long ago. Starved for attention, for someone to love her, she had married Matt in part—she now believed—

because she had jumped at the chance of building a family with
him, something that would be hers. It hadn't worked out the way
she had dreamed it would. Not by a long shot.

"The last five have felt like I'm part of a corporation planning
a takeover, not like a marriage. I haven't been happy, and I haven't
been able to figure why or what to do about it. About a year ago, I
was having dinner with my sister when this waitress started to flirt
with me." She smiled ruefully. "I didn't pick up on it at first, but
my sister did. I was like, 'she is *not* flirting,' but there was a part
of me that was intrigued. We started to chat, and next thing you
know she got my phone number. We left the restaurant and I
almost forgot about it, but the woman chased me for days, and I
was tempted to let her catch me. At the time, I was starving for
attention and flattered, and there was a part of me that thought if
it happened with a woman, it wouldn't really be unfaithful. The
flirting lasted for a few months, but I couldn't do it. Nothing happened, but I thought about it. The real eye-opener was that I
wanted to be with a woman. And I thought about what that
meant. *Could* I be with a woman? How did I feel about that? What
did it mean? Then I found out she was dating several other women
at the same time; I guess she thought I would make a good notch
for her bedpost." She laughed, but there was a hint of pain in the
soft laughter. "I did learn a lot, though. And it made me question
some things I took for granted: questions about myself, my life,
who I am, what I need to be happy. I haven't found all of the
answers yet, but I'm working on it."

Madison turned fully and fought off the urge to put her arms
around Lauren. She was truly curious as to why people stayed in
relationships after they were no longer happy. Maybe that was
why she had never been able to commit to a long-term relationship. "Why do you stay married?"

"It's complicated."

She suddenly looked so sad that Madison didn't press.

Lauren took a deep breath then slowly released it, trying to
shake off the cobwebs. "I'm taking off for our home on the Cape
on the weekend. It would be nice if...I mean, you could come."

Their eyes met and Madison sighed. There was no mistaking
the pull between them. Madison felt the heat of the attraction kin-
dle a warm fire in her stomach. "Lauren, I don't think that's such
a good idea."

Unable to stop herself, Lauren reached over and tucked a

loose strand of hair behind Madison's ear. Their eyes held. "I know, but something in you calls to me. I would like to find out what that is."

At the soft words Madison felt the ache in her midsection. "We single gals have two rules: never get involved with serial killers, and never, ever get involved with a married woman."

"Ouch!"

Madison smiled, trying to take the sting out of her words. "Let's quit while we are both ahead."

Lauren handed her a small folded piece of paper. "Here are the directions. If you change your mind, or you need to get away one day...The key is always under the blue pot by the wheelbarrow."

"Lauren..."

"Madison, I get it. But we also had a deal, remember? The offer of the getaway was real. Whenever you feel like running away, just go. We never use it until late summer. I'm just going this weekend to take a break, since Matt is going back to Washington. I need to think about some things in my life away from the pressure of being the senator's wife."

She felt like she had reached a crossroads in her life, and knew that she would need to make a decision on what that life should be. There was so much to think about and sort out. Things like: her husband wanted to be president. Things like: she wasn't in love with him. Things like: the woman beside her was stirring feelings in her she hadn't thought she would ever feel. She was thinking all of that when Madison touched her arm.

"I'm going to call it a night. Thanks for the champagne."

Lauren turned, unaware that Madison had also shifted and was closer than expected. They stood staring at each other.

Tempted, Madison took a step forward, "Lauren, I—" She broke off as she saw the dark figure crossing to them.

"There you are." Matt took his wife by the arm. "I've been looking for you. I wanted you to meet Senator Leary. He's on the Ways and Means Committee." He turned and flashed a white grin towards Madison. "Sorry to steal her away for a few minutes."

Madison smiled automatically. "It's fine. I was just going, anyway." Her smile turned to Lauren. It didn't quite reach her eyes. "See you around, Lauren."

Lauren watched her go, eyes sad. Matt continued to smile after her, his look puzzled. He had felt the tension, an awareness of having interrupted something, yet he couldn't quite place a reason for it. "You shouldn't disappear like that." There was a hint of a question behind his patented smile.

Matt's hand was warm against her elbow as he steered her back inside. Despite the heat, Lauren shivered. "I needed some air."

He studied her. "Are you okay? You look a bit pale."

"Just tired."

"We'll just stay for another hour or so, then we'll go." His hand was gentle as it touched her arm.

He can be so sweet sometimes, she thought, her heart aching. *Why can't I be in love with him?*

Chapter
Four

A gray curtain had wrapped itself around the city like a cozy blanket. The forecast called for rain and more rain. Madison, who had been staring out of the tall window in her office, placed her palm against the glass, felt the coolness against her skin. The rain battered the windows and obscured the view below. She felt the overwhelming sadness seep in through her fingertips. In a moment she would have to tell one of her oldest and dearest friend that her cancer was back, and this time there was little chance of overcoming it.

She was getting tired of the endless, losing fight. The battles won were small, and too often followed by death. By the inevitability of death. There was no cheating it. For a while, she had believed she could delay it for her patients. But even that small gesture was palling. She was tired of losing people she'd learned to care about. And that tiredness was now making her detach from everything. She was starting to feel like she was a stranger in her own life, going through the motions from a distance, unable to reengage. She was afraid of becoming one of those disinterested doctors who were unable to feel empathy. She placed her other hand against the window, as if to brace herself against the world. The door opened behind her, and she schooled her features into that calm expression that was often mistaken for aloofness by people who didn't know her.

"Hey, old girl!" The redhead burst in with unbridled energy, reminiscent of that of a puppy. It had always been irresistible. Madison smiled at her, but her eyes stayed cool, watchful.

"Hey." Kim looked at her and recognized the signs. They'd been friends for over fifteen years. There was little Madison could hide from her, even the fact that she was dying. "How long?" she asked quietly.

Madison sat down with a sigh. She should have known Kim would see right through her. The heaviness settled over her. "Six months, maybe a year. It has spread to your lymph nodes. But there are things we can do. We can try a stronger dose of..."

"No! No more chemo. I want to enjoy the months I have left, not spend them looking at the bowl of a toilet."

Madison had to smile at that. She shook her head, eyes turbulent with emotion. "I'm so sorry, Kim."

"For what?" Kim frowned at her friend. "Oh, please! If you tell me it's because you can't make me better this time, I'll have to hit you. You gave me three more years than I would have had otherwise. No one else held out any hope, but you did. You are not God, Madison. It's time you stopped taking it all on. It's not your fault when you lose the fight. You can't control life. Just help me make them the best months."

"Okay." Madison went to her and they hugged tightly.

"I need you to help me tell Jenn," Kim whispered, thinking of her partner.

Madison felt the weight of responsibility settle on her shoulders. "I will."

When the weekend came, Madison prowled around her house unable to settle in any one place. She felt restless, her entire body assaulted by nerves. When she found herself in her car, driving without any destination in mind, she knew that she was putting off what she really wanted to do. She abruptly changed direction and headed east. The drive would take less than three hours, and if she wanted to, she could turn right around and come back.

Outside of the house with its wraparound white and muted green porches and immense windows, she found herself parked without the nerve to get out. She was about to drive away when the front door opened and Lauren stepped out, a basket of wild flowers in her hand. She glanced at the car but, not recognizing it, paid it no mind, and she stepped down to go around the back when something made her turn. She never figured out what that something was. Her hand lifted to shade her eyes against the glare of the sun sparkling off the window and she stared at the car, her heart suddenly racing.

Madison hesitated as she watched the beautiful tanned woman before her. She could still leave, and it would be okay.

Instead, she opened the car door and stepped out. Lauren smiled, and they stood there grinning like fools. Then they stopped smiling and just looked at each other. The stare stretched into seconds, then moments—long, still, quiet moments on the outside, but clamorous where their emotions were housed.

For Madison, it was one of those once-in-a-lifetime-if-you're-lucky moments, the kind that even the most talented movie directors and actors can't quite capture on film. Up until then, Madison had been laboring under the misconception that such a thing didn't really exist. How could one, anyone, describe the instant when it all came together? How to describe that burst of clarity when one knew that life had just begun; that everything that had happened before could not compare to this, and that nothing would ever be the same again? She had never felt like this in her life.

"I'm sorry. I didn't know where else to go."

Lauren smiled at her, unwilling to examine the sudden feeling of giddiness that was going through her. "I'm so glad you're here. Come on in." She motioned for Madison to follow her back into the house.

Inside, Madison looked around with interest. "Wow, this is great!"

The house was all windows and wide-open spaces. In front of her, a floor-to-ceiling bank of windows looked onto the back patio and running creek. A large stone fireplace dominated the other wall. Thick rugs lay over the polished oak floors. Here and there, various pine and oak antiques were scattered. Two tall bar stools were nestled close to the airy kitchen, an inviting place to sit whiling away hours watching someone cook a meal. *She doesn't like to feel closed in,* Madison thought.

Lauren looked around and felt the same little thrill she always felt. *Mine. This is mine.* She had known the minute she saw it that this was going to be her home, not the house in Washington that reeked of subtle political showiness. She had insisted on purchasing it even when Matt disagreed. For the first time in their relationship, Lauren had ignored his calm, rational suggestion to wait till after the next election, and had bought it using her inheritance from her grandmother. That should have been a warning to her, a foreshadowing of the rebellion she was starting to feel. This was her escape, her first volley in the struggle for independence, and there was possessiveness in the look she cast around.

Her touch was everywhere: from the pictures scattered around and the abstract oil paintings on the walls to the large, open concept kitchen with its enormously efficient appliances. She loved to cook, but in Washington Matt insisted on a chef, and she was reduced to sneaking downstairs to make her avocado salads. Here, though, was her little corner of heaven. She didn't spend enough time here. But that would change. Part of her now wanted Madison to love it just as much as she did.

"Thanks. There are times when I can almost touch the moon. I love that feeling." She smiled and took hold of Madison's hand. "Come on, let's get you settled in."

They spent the day exploring the harbor, walking to the ocean and letting the salty Atlantic spray cool their heated skin. Lauren took her visitor to her favorite spot. Here, where the waves crashed like thunder and the ground was hard, was her haven against her own thoughts. This is where she came to clear her head.

"A secret place," Madison murmured.

Distracted, Lauren glanced at her. "What?"

"This," Madison gestured to the ocean, "this is a secret place." Bending, she picked up a shell, pitted by the ocean, dried like a bone in the sun. "My grandmother had this beautiful old mansion filled with antiques and silk pillows. There was a room in the attic upstairs. It was gloomy and dusty. There was a broken rocker in there and a box full of perfectly useless things. I could sit up there for hours." Bringing her gaze back to Lauren's, she smiled. "I've never been able to resist a secret place."

Lauren remembered, suddenly and vividly, a tiny room in her parents' home. When she was little, she'd closeted herself in there for hours to read and sketch. This spot had replaced it. This *was* her secret place. Lauren smiled, a part of her disturbed by how easy it was for Madison to fit into her life. She had never brought Matt here; he would never understand what it meant to her. But Madison had understood without a single word from Lauren. "So, what made you run from the city this weekend?"

Madison smiled without denying it. "You," she wanted to say, but instead spoke the other truth. "My inability to alter fate."

"Why would you want to?" Lauren asked, curious.

"So it would hurt less, I suppose."

"Ah...life wouldn't be worth living if everything was all neat and tidy, don't you think?"

Madison glanced at her, at the soft smiling curve of her mouth, and wondered what this was between them if not fate. She was also convinced that the hurting would come, and knew she was helpless to stop any of it from happening. She chose to change the subject. "I had to tell one of my oldest friend that she has only a few months to live."

"I'm sorry."

The apology nearly undid her. She'd heard those words many times before, had spoken them to countless others, but they'd never struck her with such simple sincerity. *From a stranger,* Madison thought as she turned toward the sea again. *It shouldn't mean so much coming from a stranger.* "It's all right."

They continued walking, then found a rock that jutted out over the water where they sat tossing pebbles into the rolling waves. The silence was broken intermittently by the cries of seagulls circling overhead. The two women talked about everything and nothing, and Lauren knew that she would look back on this day as one of the best days she had ever had. She enjoyed Madison's dry humor that poked fun at everything including herself, loved the quick, quirky mind that challenged her. She had never laughed so much in a day.

As the day progressed, she found herself staring at Madison, puzzled by the feelings that spending time with the dark-haired woman was causing within her. The suddenness and intensity of her feelings should have alarmed her, but they settled over her with a sense of rightness, as if it was meant to be all along. When they stopped during their walk and Madison turned to take a drink of water, Lauren stared at the curve of her neck glistening with perspiration from the heat; and without conscious thought, she stepped closer and gently blew on it.

Madison felt the soft breath against her skin, and the sensation rippled through her body. *Oh God,* she thought.

Lauren took a step back, amazed at what she had done, and blushed delicately when Madison turned to look at her. "Sorry. I don't know why I did that."

Madison's smile was strained. "That's okay."

Their eyes held, and the air seemed to vibrate with anticipation. Then Madison took another gulp of water and offered her bottle to Lauren, breaking the tension. Lauren shook her head, and they started walking again. But something had changed between them, something subtle, and for the rest of the day, Lau-

ren took every opportunity to touch Madison—often taking her
hand as they walked. Madison let her, secretly enjoying the intimacy of those moments. Over and over, their eyes met and they
exchanged long, quiet stares, trying to understand what was starting to happen between them.

Later, as Lauren was upstairs changing after dinner, Madison—tasked with finding the appropriate music—scanned the pile
of CDs. *Why, we have the same tastes,* she thought, delighted. She
discovered one in particular and stared at it, grinning foolishly.
"The Bee Gees?" she called. "I thought I was the only one that—"
She spun around as she heard footsteps behind her, her gaze land-
ing on the blond woman, then her mind went blank.

"You thought you were what?" Madison's eyes traveled up the
length of Lauren's body and back down again, the look in them
warming Lauren's skin. She felt herself heat under the stare.

"Mmm?" Madison tried to recover the part of her brain that
had gone missing. "Uh...I..." Her eyes danced over Lauren again,
unable to look away. "I don't know," she finished helplessly. Of
their own accord, her fingers brushed across the bare skin peeking
below the soft white shirt. The shirt was worn loose over the
pants, the unfastened bottom buttons showing a sexy, toned stomach.

"You like?" Lauren murmured, eyes half-closed at the touch
of Madison's fingers against her stomach.

"Oh, I like."

They stared at each other, silently accepting what their bodies
had known since the first time they had seen each other. Lauren's
eyes were as busy as Madison's, touching on every feature of her
face. That was part of her sexiness—that seemingly total absorp-
tion in whatever her eyes focused on. The intensity with which
Madison was looking at her made her feel as though her face were
the most captivating one in the world.

Everything around them faded. The sound of the water and
the breeze in the trees coming through from the open patio door
both gentled so that all that could be heard was the sound of the
womens' breathing as it quickened. Madison's mouth moved tan-
talizingly close, then paused, as if fighting against the need to possess. They stared at each other for a long moment. It was Lauren
that crossed the invisible barrier, going willingly into Madison's
arms, as eager for her kiss as the other was for hers. Her mouth
responded warmly to the thrusts of Madison's tongue that stroked

and tested and tasted until she had to pause to catch her breath.

Lowering her head, Madison pressed her face against Lauren's neck while Lauren's hands closed around the back of her head, her fingers combing through the dark hair. Madison kissed her way up to Lauren's ear. "This is crazy," she whispered.

"Very."

"Are you afraid?"

"Yes."

"Of me?"

"No."

"You should be."

"I know, but I'm not."

"Afraid of the situation?"

"Terrified," Lauren said before her mouth moved the last millimeters and dissolved against Madison's.

Madison felt her heart racing, the blood roaring in her ears. It had been so long since she had felt this strong an attraction, if ever. It was unnerving to know that her legs felt weak. She slowly pulled away, a shaking hand caressing Lauren's jaw as she watched Lauren's eyes open slowly. They stared at Madison, unfocused, arousal making them appear almost black. Madison tried to recover her sanity, her values warring with the sudden overpowering need to possess. "We can't do this," Madison whispered. "You're married."

"I know." Lauren felt completely overwhelmed, adrift, her mind empty of all rational thoughts except one: she wanted this dark-haired woman with a force that was overwhelming. She took a shaky breath. "Maybe we should just call it a night." Her body screamed in protest for the wanting of Madison's touch, and more than anything she wanted to beg and to hell with the consequences. She closed her eyes, fighting sudden tears.

"Yeah." Madison looked away, trying to regain her emotional footing on the suddenly shifting sands. She was amazed at how shaken she felt, how quickly she had lost control. She followed Lauren, and they parted ways at the top of the stairs. In the bathroom, she stared at the stranger in the mirror. She splashed cold water on her flushed face and waited until the trembling in her hands had stopped. *This was the right thing to do, but Christ, it hurt to pull away.* When she stepped out into the bedroom, Lauren was standing in the doorway, bathed in moonlight, staring at her. The hunger in her eyes reached across the room and slammed

Madison straight in the midsection, stopping her breathing.

Madison's hands clenched at her side, and she silently prayed for strength. She wanted more than anything to just cross that room and get to her. "Lauren, please go to bed. I won't be able to say no again," she whispered roughly.

Lauren stepped forward, hesitated. She looked close to tears. "Madison, I don't...I..."

Madison shook her head, then watched as the tears welled in Lauren's eyes.

Lauren was shaken; she had no frame of reference for what she was feeling. Though she knew it was wrong, she felt her need for this woman overwhelm all of her senses.

Madison was helpless against the tears. She closed the space between them and her thumb gently wiped the tears away. "Please, don't." She took a deep breath, fighting an internal battle that she lost. "You gotta promise that you will stay on your side. Okay?"

"'Kay. I promise." The two climbed into the large bed, and Lauren was as good as her word as she placed pillows between them. "Madison?"

Madison was trying hard not to move. "Hmmm?"

"I'm glad you're here. I—" She stopped.

"I know. Same goes. Go to sleep."

Madison was burning up and, still more asleep than awake, wondered when the fever had risen. The heat finally woke her up, and for a moment she was disoriented. Through the night, the two had gravitated toward each other, and now Lauren lay curled up beside her, her face buried in Madison's neck, one of her long legs thrown over Madison's, pinning her down. One of Lauren's hands had crept under Madison's T-shirt and lay against her waist, holding her. This was the heat she had been feeling. Being this close to Lauren's body was like lying beside an inferno. Madison closed her eyes, enjoying the feel of the warmth beside her, the sense of rightness. Perhaps sensing she was awake, Lauren shifted beside her, a sound close to a moan rumbling low in her throat. Her hand moved against the ribcage on which it rested, and Madison held her breath.

As she became aware of her positioning, Lauren's breathing changed against her companion's neck. She lifted her head to stare down at Madison. "Hi. Sorry." It was still dark, the moonlight filtering through the windows. She felt rather than saw Madison's smile.

"I was wondering why I felt on fire."

"Oh. Yeah." She blushed. " I...I've had complaints before. I'm a bit of a cuddler."

"Mmm. My very own little heater." Madison shifted, and in doing so caused the tanned leg to inadvertently rub up against her center. The gentle pressure brought an immediate reaction from Madison's body. She couldn't help the sudden heat that converged on one area and trembled involuntarily against the contact. She held her breath, afraid to move again.

Lauren felt her reaction and was tempted into more, without really knowing what the "more" was.

"Huh...Lauren... I think we should—oh God!" she groaned when Lauren's fingers trailed against the soft curve of her breast, a questing thumb gently tracing her nipple, which hardened and responded to the touch.

They stared at each other in the darkness. Madison nodded her head helplessly at the unspoken question in Lauren's eyes. She knew that this moment had been inevitable since the instant she had first laid eyes on the blond woman. Lauren moved on top, her body fitting over Madison's perfectly.

"We are a perfect fit," Lauren observed with a tiny smile.

Madison helped her remove her shirt and looked in awe at the firm, golden body above her. "My God, you are beautiful," she whispered, stunned.

"So are you."

Despite the swift arousal, the exploration was slow, unhurried, as they savored each touch. Their mouths toyed, teased and explored, angling this way and that way, finding their fit. In the soft, diffuse moonlight, somehow the rest of their clothing got removed, and gentle hands explored soft curves. From the open windows, the murmur of the slow-running creek interspersed with the chirping of crickets were the only sounds that broke the still night.

Unbelievingly aroused, Lauren was overwhelmed by how incredible Madison felt beneath her. "Oh God, kiss me again." Madison's mouth firmed against hers, her tongue stroking in deeply.

The long sweep of blond hair fell against Madison's face and enveloped her in the scent of Lauren's shampoo. She grabbed hold of the golden mane, pulling Lauren closer. When Madison's mouth at last closed over an already erect nipple, Lauren moaned. "You like that?" Madison's teeth gently nipped at the hardened peak.

"Yes...more," she gasped breathlessly. Lauren's fingers snaked through Madison's hair to pull her closer.

Madison's mouth trailed lower, and she delighted in the taste and the smells she found. In response to her explorations, Lauren's body shifted and pulled, her legs opening wider in a silent plea as old as time. Madison could smell Lauren's arousal, and it spurred her on. When her mouth teasingly hesitated over the soft mound, her nose tickled by the tight curls, Lauren's hips instinctively shifted higher. There was a natural seduction in the movement that caused Madison's blood to heat up to near madness. Her fingers stroked up the blonde's firm leg to the inner curve of a tight juncture, then hesitated. She was amazed at how much she could feel just with her fingertips. She was so turned on that she was afraid that she would come as soon as she touched Lauren.

When her tongue flicked against Lauren, she couldn't stop her own moan of delight at the soft, wet silk she found, and with her fingers, she gently parted the swollen folds. She could hear Lauren's husky moans, and they incited her further. She wanted to devour her, but forced herself to go slowly. She could feel the trembling in Lauren's legs as her mouth drew in some of her wetness, her tongue flicking against the sensitive skin and feeling the ripples her touch evoked. Her tongue explored the hidden softness, her senses acutely aware of every reaction Lauren was having, her ears tuned to every change in the ragged breathing of the woman above her. Slowly, she started to suck, and heard the quickening breath. There was so much heat, and Madison felt her own wetness increase in response. Her tongue stroked in deeply, and her teeth gently nipped at the hardened nub.

"Madison..." Lauren shuddered in response to Madison's tantalizing touches, stunned to realize she wouldn't last beyond a couple of strokes. She took hold of Madison's shoulders and pulled her up, and they changed positions as Madison's weight settled over her.

"Is something wrong?" Madison asked worriedly.

"No. God, no." Lauren's kiss was long and slow. Tasting herself on Madison's lips was erotic. "It just that...I'm...I just know that I am so close, and I don't want our first time to be over too quickly. I want to feel you against me when I come," she whispered. Her words echoed through Madison's body, and the doctor trembled in response.

They started moving against each other, holding on tightly, their sensitive, hardened nipples rubbing against each other. With a low groan, Lauren wrapped her legs around Madison's hips and gently pushed upwards.

Madison felt the heat and wetness against her stomach and trembled with the effort to slow down. "Oh...God...you feel so good. I don't think I can hold on," Madison groaned, feeling her body tighten, rushing to fulfillment. It was too soon, but she couldn't stop it.

"Then don't," Lauren whispered, her hands rubbing the heaving back. She was awed by how soft a woman's body was. It felt like touching silk. "I've got you."

The soft words pierced Madison's last remaining wall. Her hand lowered between them and gently she slipped one, then two fingers inside of Lauren. The blonde was so wet, and as her muscles tightened against the probing fingers, Madison's mouth found Lauren's as she felt the climax build. "Oh God, Lauren."

"Madison, look at me, " Lauren asked softly.

Madison opened her eyes and their gazes locked as they continued moving together. The pleasure on Lauren's face, the intimacy of the moment, was Madison's undoing, and she let herself go with a loud cry. As she ground herself against Lauren, she felt the blonde go rigid below her, the two of them reaching climax at almost the same instant. She collapsed, shuddering, against her as Lauren came, tightening her hold as she cried out her name. Madison floated on that, her fingers still inside Lauren.

Lauren felt as if her very soul had been touched, and her body dissolved against Madison's. They lay together, silent, the lines of their bodies touching. "Where did you come from?" she asked with a sense of wonder. Her gaze was serious; she was afraid that she would never see Madison like this again, or talk to her as she had earlier—holding nothing back.

Madison's hand caressed her jaw, her fingers trailing down Lauren's neck, feeling the shivers her touch evoked. "Maybe fate," she sighed. "I never knew what true loneliness was," she said at last, "until just now."

Lauren's eyes were grave, questioning. "I don't even know you, and yet I know you. It's like my heart recognized you from before. That's silly, huh?"

Madison hesitated, realizing that her sense of solitude, so familiar that she had come to accept it as her fate, had now become unbearable because of Lauren. Instead of answering, Madison pulled her closer, fingers buried in the thick blond hair as her mouth gentled against Lauren's. She poured all that she was feeling into the kiss. The emotion being conveyed was devastating, and it left Lauren shaken.

They lay quietly holding each other, hands unable to be still. "Madison, I want to spend more time with you." Lauren's hand trailed along Madison's neck, entranced by the curve of it.

Madison sighed. "There is so much wrong with this. But there's one thing you should know, it's not in me to be with you like this *and* to be with someone else. And someday I would need to find someone, because someday I'll want a life." She paused to give Lauren a moment to consider that, and then said, "That could hurt us both much more than stopping now."

Lauren struggled with her own emotions: a sudden swift possessiveness; a fear of loss so searing that now, at their beginning, she could only imagine it; the fierce desire to be happy. Her hand was soft against Madison's neck as she looked back at her steadily.

"I'll trust you to tell me when that is."

Madison looked away. "It could be," she answered, "the day your husband decides to run for president, because *that* would make *this* impossible." Afterward, Madison lay against her until she fell asleep.

When she awoke, it was close to morning. Everything had changed. Her thoughts were a collage: Matt and the guilt Lauren must now feel, that Madison herself felt; all that divided them— Matt's ambition, the breaching of her standards; the terrible risk if they continued. It was strange, she reflected, to believe that Lauren could sense her thoughts. She had never been a party to infidelity, and had never wished to be, and she knew without being told that neither had Lauren. Madison lay next to her, unable to sleep, afraid to speak. Lauren stirred beside her, restless. In the darkness, she felt Lauren's fingers curl around hers.

"I don't want to lose you." Lauren curled against her, her lips finding Madison's again.

For Madison, there was no going back. She could not turn the page on what was done. She had fallen hard, and now the need grew in her to quiet the disquiet that arose from being part of betrayal. She turned to Lauren. "Tell me about Matt."

The next few days passed in a blur of exploration and wonder for the new lovers—hours spent just staring at each other, talking long into the night, sharing the innermost parts of one another. On the last day, Madison went for a run along the rough coast. Without being told, Lauren understood her need for solitude and let her go.

The last couple of nights had brought a desperate quality to their being together, as if they were trying to make the most of every moment. Returning from her run feeling more lost than before, Madison was paralyzed by the magnificent vision of Lauren wading effortlessly through the water as she fished, casting her line with graceful movements almost like a dance, muscles in her arms rippling each time she flicked the line with her wrist. She opened her mouth, but nothing came out, and she just looked helplessly at Lauren, wishing something, anything, would be adequate to describe what the mere sight of this woman did to her.

"Hey?" Lauren's brows furrowed when she saw the expression on Madison's face. "Are you all right?"

"Yeah," she said, blushing furiously. "I just..." She smiled as she walked to her. "You just look so beautiful. Sometimes when I look at you," she confessed softly, "I can't breathe. You have no idea of what just looking at you does to me."

"If it's anything like what looking at you does to me, then I think I've got a pretty good idea." Lauren's look was soft. "I like the way you look at me, the picture of me you seem to hold in your head."

"You take my breath away, Lauren. So much so that it scares me at times."

Touched by the words, Lauren kissed her, her mouth gentle.

Chapter
Five

Month by month, a year passed. Lauren and Madison came to need each other's company, each other's thoughts. Sometimes days went by without them seeing one another. Sometimes, when Lauren had to travel to Washington to be with Matt at some function or other, a week or more might pass. But every day they would talk on the phone. As if by tacit understanding, the subject of their future was never brought up. Often they would talk about the past, Madison—with the directness of an old friend—questioning Lauren regarding Matt, their marriage. She had never felt so close to anyone. Whenever she needed Lauren to listen, she was there, whether it was about a patient or Kim's declining health or the harsh demands of their affair.

"When you're away," she told Lauren after a few months, "I think about you with Matt. Even though you say you never sleep with him."

Lauren's look was gentle, querying. "Would you be with me if you could be?"

Madison shook her head, feeling the words squeeze at her heart. "How can I answer that?"

By unspoken consent, their days were spent in the present, and in the present, there was little they didn't share. But often they just made each other smile.

At every opportunity they snuck away to the Cape, and it became their oasis—their own private little corner of heaven, where nothing could touch them. Here, they felt like a couple. They could live without worry. Unconstrained by the demands of everyday life or the need to hide, they enjoyed their carefree time together. From the window, no one could see them.

On one such occasion, they lay naked in the sunlight, unhurriedly touching as they looked into each other's faces. Madison traced a finger along the firm stomach. *I'm in love with you,* she thought with sadness. *I'll never love anyone this much again.*

Lauren kissed her fingers and smiled at her. "Honey, maybe we should go for a walk; you know, get some fresh air, exercise."

Madison tried to shake her mood and smiled back at her.

Lauren's eyes were intent now, questioning. "What is it?"

"Nothing," Madison murmured.

Lauren kissed her throat, her tongue tasting the salty skin. *Would a life for us be possible if Matt never went beyond the Senate?* Lauren wondered. *Can two women really make a go of it and live their lives together?* She wanted it with the fierce desire of someone who has been starved for too long, but right on the heels of that desire was the white-hot fear of the unknown. *Could I destroy Matt's chances for my own chance at happiness?* "Maddie?"

"Mmm?"

"Would you, I mean, could you see a life with me?"

"What are you saying, Lauren?"

Lauren looked at her and knew that Madison was so much a part of her that she didn't want to ever let her go. She felt the weight of her marriage press down on her chest. "Give me time," she answered, "to sort things out."

"You remember Lauren?" Alex waved toward Lauren, who stood by the kitchen doorway, a glass of wine in her hand. Dressed in a short green dress with her long blond hair falling in waves to her shoulder, she looked stunning.

Madison, who had just finished hugging her friend, turned in surprise, and her breath caught at the sight. She hadn't known that Lauren was going to be at Alex's fortieth birthday party.

"Yes, hello." Lauren smiled at her slowly, the look in her eyes immediately stirring Madison's blood. "Surprise," Lauren mouthed at her.

Madison shook her head, trying to clear it. It had been three weeks since she had seen her lover, and the sight of her standing across the room had her grinning goofily. She crossed to Lauren, hugging other friends along the way. "I thought you were the keynote speaker at some conference?"

"Yeah, well...I came down with the flu. Funny how that happens. Timing is everything," Lauren added with a quiet smile. Her look was soft. "I've missed you."

"I missed you, too," Madison returned, fighting the urge to touch her.

"Hey, you two, come and see this new game!" Jamie yelled out.

At the dinner table, Madison found herself sitting beside Lauren. The soft scent of sandalwood drifted over her, and she felt her body responding to the blond woman's nearness. As she toyed with the food on her plate, she half listened to the numerous conversations going on around her, distracted by Lauren's presence. When she felt a soft hand on her knee, she started. Her eyes widened as the gentle fingers stroked up her thigh. She glanced at Lauren from the corner of her eye, but Lauren was talking to the woman beside her. When the fingers inched up closer to the heat spreading between her legs, Madison closed her eyes against the torture. Her hand reached under the table to stop the progress of the dangerous digits as she leaned close to Lauren and whispered in her ear, "Be good."

Lauren turned to her and her smile was wicked. "I'm always good," she whispered back, her breath dancing over Madison's ear and sending shivers down her spine.

Darcy, one of Madison's closest friends, watched the interplay between the two with puzzled interest. Something didn't seem quite right.

Madison took a sip of her wine at about the same time that cool fingers slipped in the gap between her shorts and her skin to touch her. She moaned as she felt the soft stroking. Eyes turn to her in amusement. Madison blushed and lifted her glass. "This is a really great wine," she told the interested onlookers. She frowned at Lauren in warning, meeting her dancing eyes with a faint smile. Lauren was driving her crazy, and she knew that if the woman touched her again, she would come right there at the table with about forty of her friends watching her, or else she would surely die from the teasing. *But what a way to go!* The rest of the dinner passed in a haze of arousal.

Lauren shifted, feeling her own wetness increase just from seeing Madison respond beside her. What had started as teasing play had turned on her. She was just as excited as her victim and felt the unrelenting pressure between her legs, her nipples rubbing almost painfully against her dress.

After dinner, as everyone spread out through the house once again, Madison watched as Lauren left the room. Distracted, she missed Darcy's question. Darcy studied her, trying to understand why her instincts were setting off warning bells.

Madison excused herself and followed Lauren up the stairs, looking for her. When she noticed the closed bathroom door, she hesitated in front of it, just as the door opened. Lauren stood staring at her, lips parted, her eyes heating up, then with a swift move, she pulled Madison in, closing the door behind her. Her mouth found the dark-haired woman's with frantic urgency, and she groaned as their bodies connected.

"God, I've missed you," she moaned, as Madison nipped then sucked on her bottom lip. "I can't wait." Her fingers slid beneath clothing and entered Madison, and as she felt the heated wetness, she almost exploded.

Madison shoved her against the door, her own fingers entering Lauren, her thumb stroking the hardened tip. Her leg fitted itself between Lauren's, supporting her weight as her fingers stroked deep.

Lauren closed her eyes as her fingers matched Madison's rhythm. As her orgasm started, she cried out, unable to stop herself. Madison's mouth found hers again, swallowing her cries as she took her over the top, falling over at the same time with rolling waves of heat. They collapsed against the door, panting, trying to catch their breath.

Lauren slowly opened her eyes and with a trembling hand stroked the hair from Madison's damp forehead. "You drive me crazy," she whispered. "All I think about is you."

Madison kissed her. "Same goes."

Later, Madison poured a glass of wine and looked out the window, a pensive look on her face. When she heard a scrape, she half turned and glanced sideways at Darcy, who had entered the kitchen. She smiled at her. "Want some?"

"Sure." Darcy leaned against the counter with crossed arms and watched Madison pour the red liquid in another glass. "How long have we known each other?" Darcy asked suddenly, the look in her eyes watchful, concerned.

"What? Forever. Probably too long," Madison answered with a grin. She handed her friend a glass and gently tapped it in a toast. "Cheers."

"Probably." Darcy gently rolled the glass between her fingers, watching the ruby wine swirl against the curved side of the glass.

Madison could see something was worrying her friend, whose forehead was creased by a faint frown. "What's up, Darcy?"

Hesitating for a moment, Darcy shoved her hand through her thick auburn curls, then sighed. "Don't take this the wrong way, 'cause I am speaking as a friend, but you're playing with fire. Just...just be careful, okay?"

Madison turned to her. "What are you talking about?"

"Lauren. Be careful you're not being used as an experiment."

Madison looked at her, stunned by the implications of her warning, then felt the slow burn of resentment. "It's none of your business, Darcy."

"I know." Darcy looked at her for a beat. "I just...I just love you, and I don't want to see you hurt." It had disaster written all over it, and her worry was for her friend—who never fell easily, but once she did, gave it her all.

Madison sighed. "I know. But it's too late for advice. I'm in love with her."

Darcy's eyes focused on the ceiling. She had been afraid of that. "Fuck." She sipped her wine, digesting the news. "How does she feel about you?"

"I don't know. The same, I think..." Madison frowned. "I've never felt like this in my life. She fits me. Here." She tapped her chest. She smiled, but there was sadness in her smile. She didn't know how long she could keep living a double life, loving in secret. She missed Lauren more each day, and was having trouble concentrating on her work and her life without her lover near. She dismissed the uncertainty of their future with a sigh.

"Fuck."

"You say 'fuck' too much." Madison's arms went around her friend. "Thanks for caring, Darcy. I love you, too. Don't worry about it. Everything will work out."

"I hope it works out the way you want it to, Maddie." She had her doubts, but refrained from saying anything more.

At around ten, most of the partygoers had slowly dispersed, leaving only a few stragglers behind. Alex sat on the couch, her arm around her new girlfriend. "Why don't you stay here?" she asked Lauren, who had started making noises about going to a hotel. "You usually do."

"Yeah, I know, but I have a really early flight to catch. It will be easier to be near the airport."

"I'll drive you," Madison volunteered quickly in the silence. Lauren met her eyes, and something in her look took Madison's breath away. *God, she keeps looking at me like that, and I'm going to turn into a puddle.* It took them several minutes to say goodbye, as everyone insisted on hugs and kisses, but they finally made it out, almost running to the car. In the car, Madison turned the key in the ignition, then looked over as Lauren reached out to take her hand.

"Hello."

"Hello back."

"I really do have an early flight to catch."

"I know."

"Maybe we can spend the whole night awake. I don't want to miss any of the hours we have left by sleeping."

Madison smiled at her. "Okay."

Lauren lifted her hand and kissed her knuckles. "You're so beautiful."

Startled, Madison looked at her with a shy smile. She would never understand what she had done right, but somehow her life had started to make sense the day she'd met Lauren. "Somebody up there must really like me," she muttered.

"What was that, honey?"

"Nothing; let's get you to that hotel."

They dozed off despite their best efforts, unable to completely fight off the exhaustion they both felt. They slept wrapped in each other's arms, waking up throughout the night to gently rub a back, or touch a shoulder, almost as if to reassure each other they were still there. As the light started to creep through the partially opened blinds, Madison lay awake with Lauren curled beside her. Her hand gently rubbed Lauren's bare shoulder, then her silky smooth back, unable to be still. It was at moments like these that she felt the intensity of her feelings for Lauren most strongly.

Those moments when everything was quiet and still, and she was left to marvel at what they had found despite the odds. She felt such peace when she was with Lauren. It made their separations more acute. Lying beside her, she felt the gentle rise and fall of her lover's breathing, and knew that she didn't want to move ever again. "You make me feel so safe," she whispered as she kissed the top of the blond head.

Lauren, who had awakened, leaned up on her arm to look down at her with a sleepy smile. "Do I?"

Madison smiled back. "Yeah."

Lauren looked at her searchingly, the probing intensity of her stare almost painful. She suddenly knew with a startling clarity that this woman was it for her. "I'm crazy in love with you, Madison."

It was the first time that those words had been spoken, and for a long moment, their eyes held, and then Lauren smiled, breaking the tension. "So, there you go."

Madison continued to stare at her, tears filling her eyes. "You have no idea how long I've been wanting to tell you that."

"That I'm in love with you?" Lauren kissed her shoulder, her mouth, traveled along the curve of her neck.

"No, silly. Me. I'm in love with you. Have been since the first day I laid eyes on you."

"Really?" Lauren smiled in delight. "How about that? I fell in love with the curve of your neck that day you came to the Cape. All I could think about was kissing it. It's the sexiest thing I've ever seen."

Having promised Lauren that she would fly out to Washington during the week, Madison got ready to drive her to the airport later that morning. She was tucking her shirt into her jeans when she glanced into the open door of the bathroom. She watched Lauren through the frosted shower glass—head back, water cascading down on her. The sight almost brought her to her knees. She crossed back into the bathroom, silently opened the glass door, and still fully clothed, stepped in. Lauren jumped, startled out of her daydreaming. Without saying a word, Madison fused her mouth to Lauren's, her hands brushing over the golden body, finding all of the sensitive spots. One hand rubbed an already erect nipple as her jean-clad leg parted Lauren's legs, pressing her back against the wet tiles. Her fingers entered Lauren, finding the exquisite heat and wetness, and she took her over the top quickly, her lover's teeth tightening against her shoulder as the water poured down on them. Not one word was exchanged.

After their long evening of sex, Lauren hadn't thought that she had anything left. But the heat from Madison's mouth as it ravaged her body and the deep stroke of Madison's fingers had her coming with a long, long cry, holding on to Madison's shoulders as she felt her legs give way, her body liquefied. Eyes closed, swollen mouth throbbing, she would have fallen in a heap if her weight hadn't been supported by Madison. "Where did that come from?"

Madison smiled into the curve of her neck breathing in her scent. "The sight of you sometimes sends me over the edge, and I just need to take you. Is that okay?"

Lauren opened her eyes. There was no blood flowing to her brain; it had drained away at the heat that came from Madison's fingers. She felt scattered, shattered, and utterly blessed. "'Kay." This was turning out to be a great day.

Chapter Six

"Are you certain?" At the answer, Lauren hung up without saying goodbye. One phone call, that was all it took to shatter her plans, her dreams of the future. Her mind swirled with a thousand thoughts but could not grab hold of a one. Something that should have filled her with joy now filled her with dread and hopelessness. She stared down at her hand, puzzled. Those same shaking fingers had only hours ago been filled with Madison. The thought of Madison brought pain searing through her stomach, and she doubled over as the nausea rose. Now that she had finally tasted the joy of being head over heels in love, how could she face the loss of that love?

When Madison arrived at her office to meet her for lunch, Lauren stared at her, unable to process any of her thoughts. She started to shake as Madison put her arms around her, and the tremors intensified when Madison's hold tightened, signaling her alarm.

"Honey, what's wrong?"

Lauren's eyes filled with tears, and she felt her heart break all over again for the pain she was about to cause.

Madison started to panic. "What is it? What's going on?"

"I got the results from my physical," Lauren started, looking away.

"Should I sit down?" At Lauren's nod, Madison sat. She had doubts that her legs would have continued supporting her anyway. Thoughts wrapped around inside her mind. She couldn't focus on any. The only clear thought that kept reappearing was fear: somehow, she was losing Lauren.

"Madison, I'm pregnant."

It could have been anything. The words themselves didn't register. The sense of relief came first; then the realization of what that meant hit her. "Pregnant..." That meant that Lauren was still sleeping with Matt. The stab of betrayal made her flinch. Still, it was ironic that she—who was a party to unfaithfulness—could feel betrayed.

All of those feelings were easily read on her face. Each one was a wound to Lauren's heart. "Honey, I'm so sorry..." She tried to cross to her, but Madison jumped up and backed away.

"Does Matt know?"

"No."

Madison turned, unable to look at Lauren. "Well, that's something."

"It happened only the one time. I felt guilty and I—"

"You don't owe me an explanation, Lauren. After all, you are married. I don't really have a right to be upset, do I?"

"Madison, I'm so sorry I lied."

Madison felt the pain deep in her core. "I'm sorry, too."

"I don't know how to fix it." Lauren's face reflected her anguish. "I don't want to be with him, I want to be with you."

Madison flinched. She closed her eyes against the hurt on Lauren's face, the plea in her eyes, then opened her eyes again to look at her. "Then leave him. Now. Come with me; give us a chance. If you do, I promise that I will spend our days together showing you how cherished you are, how much you matter." Her voice broke with the emotion.

Lauren felt her heart squeeze; the hurt and conflict lay bare on her face. "I'm going to leave him. I just need some time to sort things out."

How much time? When will it stop? When you are in the White House? Madison knew with absolute clarity that she had no pride when it came to Lauren. She would be willing to compromise everything that she was and everything that she believed in. Already had. But at what cost to the both of them? She also knew instinctively, in that moment, that Lauren was fundamentally incapable of making a choice that involved hurting someone she cared for, and that to survive, Madison would have to be the one to leave.

Madison's hand touched Lauren's cheek, gently memorizing her face. "From the very beginning, I realized I was drawn to you more than to anyone in my life. And I came to trust you, to feel you were the person I could say anything to and still be understood. I felt that before I ever made love with you. After that, the feeling was like a hunger, so deep that it scared me even more. I knew we had to end, should end, but I kept making deals with myself, stealing hours, days, weeks."

She let her hand linger against Lauren's jaw, as if unable to break the connection. Lauren turned her head to kiss the inside of her palm, lips soft against her skin. Madison felt the sweetness of the gesture rip through her. She stepped away as the hurt spread. "If you could leave him, you would have done it before this. I don't believe in ultimatums, Lauren. You have to live the life you were meant to live, and only you know what that is. You and Matt have been waiting for this moment forever—to have a family. How can I stand in the way of that? But I can't live with the lies and the sneaking around anymore. I don't much like myself, what being with you has forced me to be. This pregnancy might be a sign that it's time for us to walk away." She wouldn't cry; once she began she'd never stop. Instead, she stood very stiff, as if to ward off the blow, and tried desperately to get her legs to move toward the door.

Lauren made a move to go to her, but Madison lifted her hand as if to fend her off. "Don't. Please, don't. I'm not strong enough. I just can't do this anymore; I have to go." She turned toward the door.

Lauren felt like she was shattering into tiny jagged pieces. "Madison, don't...don't leave. Please. Please. I just need time to..." She was crumbling inside, and yet she was still standing.

Madison stopped at the door, her face averted so that Lauren could not see the utter devastation she was feeling. She took a deep breath and turned to give her one long, last look.

Lauren stood crying, unable to comprehend what it all meant. Inside she felt like she was dying a slow death.

"Timing is everything in life. I guess this just wasn't our time. Giving you up is the hardest thing I have ever done in my life. Lauren, I...If you ever need anything, you just have to call." Her voice broke on the last word, her throat raw and tight. Without waiting for a reply, Madison let herself out. The door shut with a click that seemed louder for the finality of the moment.

Chapter
Seven

"Typical, lying around till noon."

Madison heard the voice dimly through sleep, recognized it, and groaned. "Oh, Christ, go away, Alex."

"Nice to see you, too." With apparent glee, Alex gave the drape cord an enthusiastic tug and sent sunlight lasering into her friend's eyes.

"I've always hated you." In self-defense, Madison pulled a pillow over her face. "Go pick on someone else."

"I took the afternoon off just so I could pick on you." In her efficient way, she sat on the edge of the bed and snatched the pillow out of Madison's hands. Concern was masked behind an appraising eye. "You don't look half bad."

Madison pried open one eye, saw the smile and shut it again. "Go away."

"If I go, the coffee goes."

"Coffee?"

"Mm-hmm. And croissants."

"Okay, you can stay." Madison sat up and held her hand out for the cup of coffee. She took a long sip. "How did you know where I would be?"

Alex studied her a while. "Darcy called and told me you showed up last night and went straight to bed." She didn't mention that she had also said that Madison had been hysterical. "Want to tell me what happened?"

Madison sighed. "I messed up real bad this time. I have no idea how to fix it."

Alex continued to watch her, saying nothing.

"I went and fell in love with Lauren. Madly. Completely. Hopelessly. And it makes no sense. And the worst part is, she is now pregnant." Tears welled in her eyes, and she started to cry.

Alex hid her shock. *Madison and Lauren?* She should have known something was up. For months Lauren had been evasive, Madison distracted. *But Lauren and Madison?* "Hey. Don't do that!" Alex said in panic. Cool under pressure, she collapsed when confronted with tears. She was a sympathetic crier, unable to stop herself from crying whenever someone she cared about cried. "I'm so sorry, honey."

"I don't know what to do. I don't know how to recover from this. It's like waking up after sleeping for years and feeling everything more acutely, seeing everything so much brighter. The colors are more beautiful, the joy more intense, the pain more unbearable. I don't know how I can put the pieces of my life back together again."

The night before, alone in her room, Madison could not stop crying. It was as if all her strength had been for that brief moment when she had walked out of Lauren's office. In place of the things she had said, she imagined having told Lauren, "I love you. I want to be with you." Imagined it a thousand times, after it was too late. Imagined being selfish, no matter what the cost. Imagined it again now, like a child who did not like the story she had heard, who wished to change the ending. Except that it was their story, Lauren's and hers, and she had written the ending herself.

Alex stroked her head. "I am so very sorry."

Madison smiled sadly. "I'm in love with her, and I know with absolute certainty that I'll never love anyone this much again. I just wish it didn't hurt so damn bad." *As time passes, memory fades; and it is both a blessing and a curse.* She hoped to hell whoever had written that was right; she had no idea how she would go on without Lauren in her life.

"She doesn't deserve your love." Alex was reacting to the hurt on Madison's face. She was and would always be a fiercely protective friend. Right at that moment, her shock at hearing about Madison's involvement with Lauren was tempered by her concern for Madison. The next day her concern and worry would be for the both of them.

"I don't think that's for you to say."

"Madison, I know it hurts, but maybe this is for the best. She has not left her husband, and she is pregnant. That should tell you where her head is at."

"I hear what you're saying, but this...pregnancy thing is different for her. And it has shaken her up just as much as it did me."

"How can you know?"

"Because a person can fuck anyone, but she loves only one: me."

"You believe that?"

"I have to." The gray eyes swirled with images, feelings. "I have to," she whispered. How else could she stay sane? To believe that all of this had happened as just an affair would cheapen everything, cause her to doubt her sanity.

Alex's new girlfriend Megan, who had been standing silently in the doorway, glanced at Alex, who was about to speak, and frowned. Taking the hint, Alex didn't pursue the issue, just commiserated. "I'm so sorry, honey."

Later in their room, Alex turned to Megan. "Why did you stop me?"

"Alex, I know you hurt for your friend, but she feels awful enough without us piling more hurt on top."

"Wait until I talk to Lauren. I'll—"

"You'll nothing." Megan's tone was firm. "You weren't there. You don't know what Lauren was going through, *is* going through. It's easy to sit in judgment, especially when someone we love is hurt, but we just don't know what really happened."

Alex sighed. Megan was right. What did she know? "It's just that I've never seen her like this. She is so broken; it's like a part of her has died. Lauren should leave Matt. Hell, she should have left him years ago when she started to have feelings for that other stupid girl. I mean, she has been unhappy for years. Why the hell stay with the jerk?"

"Leaving a relationship is never easy, for a number of reasons. You of all people should know this." Alex and Samantha had been going through the motions for years prior to Sam's death, and Alex, under different circumstances, would have readily admitted that leaving something familiar was often harder than just staying.

Megan smiled at her new lover, touched by Alex's fierce protectiveness towards her friends. "Sometimes you can meet someone, and it is never meant to last. The intensity of the feelings is too strong to survive; it burns too brightly. Maybe the fit is *too* right. Like once you find your true soulmate, you can't survive it. I don't know. Life has a way of blowing up on people for a multitude of reasons. Most of all, when we love."

They got ready for bed and, as was habit, Megan turned the

TV on to CNN for the latest news. When a clip with breaking news interrupted, Megan—fluffing up her pillows—didn't pay attention until the name was repeated. "Oh, my God!" Megan stared at the screen, horrified. "Alex?"

Alex poked her head out of the bathroom. "Hmm?" She turned to the screen as the news was repeated.

They stared at each other. "Do we tell her?"

Megan shook her head. "I don't know. What good can come of it?"

"Senator, Senator, will this affect your plans? Will this stop you from running?"

The questions came at Matt fast and furious as he paused in the doorway of the hospital. His face was pale, his hair tousled, and the image of the handsome young senator rushing to his wife's bedside would play well on the evening news. That no one, including him, had known about the baby was irrelevant now.

Watching him, Keith McGraw shook his head. The Democratic Party's best hope, looking appropriately grave and concerned, paused at the door to throw a serious look at the group of reporters huddled in the rain. He was still politician enough to choose to go in through the main doors where he knew the reporters had camped out. This couldn't have been better planned. *Talk about luck*, Keith thought, amused at his cynicism. He tuned in to Matt's words.

"Right now, my priority is to be by my wife's side and make sure she is okay. Any other thoughts have quite obviously been put on the back burner."

Keith smiled. "Lucky bastard. His wife miscarries just before he announces his candidacy. He couldn't have planned it better."

Another reporter by his side snickered. "Aren't we cynical."

Keith shrugged. "I'm just stating the obvious. He couldn't have asked for a better start to his campaign. Just think of the sympathy votes he will be getting."

Inside the hospital, some of those same thoughts were being considered by Clarence Lyons, Matt's campaign manager. He was disappointed that there would be no baby, but his focus was on making the most of it. It was also time to put his cards on the table. He made his way to Lauren's room.

Inside, Lauren lay broken, weak from the large amount of

blood loss during hemorrhaging. Before losing consciousness, half delirious, she had pleaded and screamed for Madison over and over again, begging for them to find her. No one knew who Madison was, and the only person they contacted was Matt in Washington. Still, for a while she had half expected to see Madison appear at the door, but as the hours passed, she realized with heartbreaking certainty that she would not. When the door opened, she barely glanced over. The large hulking form of Clarence had her closing her eyes.

She looked so pale and fragile against the white sheet that he hesitated. He waited by her bedside until she opened her eyes again. "Hi." She stared at him silently. "Lauren, I'm so sorry for your loss."

She closed her eyes, feeling the pain spear through her. *The baby.* She'd had almost no time to get used to the idea. The loss was as searing as it was heartbreaking, both because of the baby, and because she had needlessly given up the love of her life.

Clarence looked uncomfortable. "Lauren, believe me when I say that I'm even more sorry for this." He placed a large brown envelope beside her on the bed. When she made no move to look at it, he opened it and pulled out the photos and placed them on her lap.

Lauren's eyes flickered down to the black-and-white pictures. She knew the exact spot where those pictures had been taken, felt the touch of Madison's hand on her face as if she were right there. But she was not. She closed her eyes, despair overwhelming her.

"Want to talk about it?"

"No."

"It would be best if this ended, Lauren."

"Best for whom?"

"Best for everyone. What were you thinking? That you could just walk off into the sunset and live happily ever after, playing the lesbian? That's not you, Lauren. Think of Matt's future, your future. You've had your fling. Hell, we all make mistakes. But now it's time to focus on the campaign. You know Matt represents the party's best hope, maybe even the country's. But we need you on board. He needs you. Don't make the mistake of thinking that this little encounter is more than it is or can be. Don't ruin your future because you were bored and I've kept Matt too busy. We can fix that. You just need to put this little adventure behind you. No one needs to know. There are a lot of people who have invested in this candidacy. Not just you, but everyone who's sacrificed career and money and time with their family to make this work. Do you want to destroy Matt's chances? Do you care so little for him? What about your own career? If this ever got out, do you really think you could still be taken seriously as a journalist? Think of all the good you could do as first lady."

Lauren looked at him, feeling hatred for him and all he represented. The hatred was also for Matt and his ambition, but most of it was self-directed. She hadn't had the guts or the strength to walk away when she could have. Two years ago, when she knew that she had stopped being in love with Matt and had recognized her attraction to a woman, she should have left then, when the presidency was only a gleam in Matt's eyes. Now he was committed to it, the party troops mobilized. Falling in love with Madison had turned her world upside down and given her a glimpse of what life could be, and now it was too late. She hadn't considered then the thought that one day she would be faced with a choice between helping a man she still deeply loved, whom she considered family, and her own happiness. Was it selfish to want more out of life than what she had? What was it that she wanted? If only Madison could have waited for her to figure things out.

She glanced at the pictures and felt the raw hurt spread. Madison had left her. And now she could see her future path, and it led straight to the White House. Too exhausted and weak to fight it any longer, she felt the hurt spread through her body as she gave in to the inevitability of her life. "Fine. You win." She turned her face away.

Clarence watched the devastation on her face and felt a twinge of guilt, quickly buried. He took the photos and let himself out. They had a campaign to prepare.

Chapter
Eight

Back to the present

Keith reread the therapist's notes. His job was not a simple one. Fairly often some politician accused him of betrayal. But he could not readily imagine ending someone's chance to be president, especially because of something the candidate's wife had done. Far less had Keith conceived of destroying a friend for something that was at its heart as private as, judging from this document, it was shattering. But what unsettled Keith most were not his personal reservations, but another of those unavoidable truths—his own rush of excitement at the start of what could be *the* political story of almost any journalist's career. Keith hunched inside the doorway with his cell phone.

His editor Bill Kaiser spoke as loudly as he could. "So?"

"She denied it."

"Of course she denied it. Really, what did you expect?" He didn't wait for a reply. "It's a killer story, with two big questions: can we source it; and if we can, will we decide to print it?"

Keith could already imagine the heated meetings between the various editors and the publisher to approve every move, including the decision as to whether *Newsbeat* should change the course of an as yet undeclared campaign.

"We need sources. We need to send someone to knock on this therapist's door and force her to go on record. We then need to find this Madison Williams. And as a last resort, we need to go to the candidate himself and pose the question whether or not he knew that his wife was screwing around...with another woman."

Keith could picture the ambush and felt a momentary sense of disgust. "Right. I'll get right on that."

After Keith's visit, Lauren lay on the bed, the wounds

reopened. Even after months of not thinking about Madison, it had taken just this visit to bring it all back. She could still close her eyes and the image was as clear as if she had seen her lover only the day before. Her voice, a gentle huskiness that never failed to bring Lauren to her knees, was still loud in her head.

How could life be so cruel as to make her fall in love with someone she could not have, and then years later make her revisit it all again? Even now she wondered how she could have let Madison walk away. She had felt like such a coward. In fact, she was a coward still. Her chance at happiness had slipped out of reach two years before, and she had barely fought for it.

She knew that she had lost a piece of herself the moment Madison had walked out, and she could never get that part back. She would never completely recover. A part of her soul had been left behind. Too afraid that she would not be able to come back from the hurt, she hadn't cried since that time in the therapist's office. With time, a thin veneer had grown over the hurt, but now and then she could still feel the ache below the facade.

She could rant and rail against fate, but she had put herself out there, knowing full well what the outcome could be. In all likelihood, should be. She had only herself to blame for that. How could it have had any other ending? The guilt had been overwhelming at the time. Now it was more a quiet desperation that filled her whenever she examined her life too closely. She wore the sheer weight of her unhappiness like a comfortable blanket, more familiar to her than those months of happiness. But she would be damned if she would stand by and let it explode years later, hurting the two people she had tried to protect. Not now. Not after two years. She was sure Madison had moved on, and she did not deserve to have her life splashed all over the news because she had had the misfortune to fall for a married woman four years before.

What if Madison is *in a new relationship?* She didn't want to think about that one thought too closely. She knew that Keith would not give up the hunt, and if it wasn't Keith, it would be someone else. Her mind clicked into gear. She walked over to the telephone and dialed a number. "We need to talk."

When Clarence entered, Lauren acknowledged the same brief flare of anger that was always there whenever he was around. Though she knew that Matt depended on him more than on anyone else, she had never been able to get past that night in the hospital and what he had asked her to do. But now she also knew that she would need him to use that same single-mindedness and ruthless thinking if they were to have any hope of surviving the scandal. "We have a problem."

For twenty minutes, Clarence listened. When Lauren finished telling her tale, he noted that her face was ashen. "You believe it's this therapist?"

"Or someone with access to her files. I was such a wreck, she could have been anyone."

"Do you want me to tell him?"

She looked at him. It would be so easy to let him do the dirty work, regardless of the spin he would put on it, but that was the coward's way. She had been a coward for too long. She shook her head. "No, I'll tell him. But, Clarence, this is the last time you and I will mention this. Ever."

"Give me twenty-four hours to meet with the team to formulate a plan. I know he will need one." He stood up, his bulk intimidating in the tiny study.

"Clarence?" When he turned, she warned, "Don't even dream of going to her or going after her, or I'll break this story myself. I swear to God."

His look was suddenly hard. She stared back at him, equally resolved. He nodded once, then left.

Chapter Nine

"Madison Williams?" The nurse in the reception area scanned the internal phone list. "Nah. Can't find anyone by that name here. Are you sure she is staff?"

Keith shrugged. After a week of searching for Madison, he had stumbled on a small article and picture of Lauren and Madison taken at some fundraiser around the time of the alleged affair. Now he had played a hunch and gone to the hospital mentioned in the article. "I thought she was." He smiled.

The woman glanced once more through the list. "Sorry. Can't find anyone here by that name. We've got about 17 Williamses, but no Madison."

He left the desk and crossed to the bank of pay phones. He was about to dial when his eyes caught the interested look of the security guard sitting at the desk. The old man was flipping through the sport pages and occasionally looking up at Keith. He looked as ancient as the furniture, and for an amused moment Keith wondered how this decrepit fellow could secure anything.

"Can I help you?"

"I hope so. I lost touch with someone I used to go to school with, and was hoping to reconnect somehow. She worked here about two years ago."

The guard leaned back in his chair, the movement causing his uniform to stretch dangerously over his inflated stomach. Buttons could pop at any moment. "What's the name?"

"Madison Williams."

He scratched his belly pensively. "Madison, Madison...New York!"

Keith had known it was a long shot, and was about to thank him and move on.

"Oh yeah, I remember the doc. She's a doctor, right?"

"Oh...yeah."

"She's a beauty. She worked the cancer ward up on the sixth floor, but she left about two years ago. She always said hello. We used to joke about her name. I used to call her New York, and..."

"Any idea where she went? Did she transfer to another hospital, maybe?" Keith interrupted, suddenly impatient.

He picked at his nose. "Can't say. All I know is, she left. You know, she didn't even say goodbye."

After thanking him, Keith walked out. He felt the excitement of the chase. It was a lead, at least. She was, or had been, a doctor. He grabbed his cell and called the office. "I need a favor," he said without preamble. "Who do we know on the medical board?"

Chapter
Ten

"Jesus," Tom Reynolds, Matt's security specialist, murmured.

It was seven o'clock. Clarence sat in his hotel suite with Tom, Heather Parker, the communication lead, John Smythe, their pollster, and two pots of coffee. Tom's voice was the first sound since Clarence had finished speaking. Now there was a long pause as Clarence watched each of them collect their thoughts and sort out the pieces: the therapist's memo; Keith McGraw's visit to Lauren; Lauren's denial. No one had asked if the allegation was true. Clarence was not surprised. Everyone just went on the assumption that it was. They were like defense attorneys who never asked if the client was guilty, only whether there was any concrete evidence. The gloom was palpable.

It was John Smythe who spoke next. "Well," he said, "this could gain us the gay votes we kissed goodbye after the last election."

No one smiled. Heather's face was strangely calm. Frankly, Clarence had expected more shock from her, as she was the one who would be out there directly in the line of fire, answering the questions.

Carefully, she asked Clarence, "Does Matt know?"

Clarence shook his head. "Not yet. She was giving us a day to plan something, then she was going to tell him."

"Poor Lauren." Her face reflected sympathy.

After another few moments of silence, it was Heather who again spoke. "Besides the memo, is there any other solid proof, aside from someone who thinks they saw or heard something?"

Clarence thought of the pictures. He looked at Tom, who was the only other person who knew about them. He shrugged. "At this point, who knows?"

"What about this woman?" John Smythe asked. "The therapist who gave up the notes? Can we send someone to talk to her?"

Clarence gave a curt shake of the head. "That would make her look more credible. If *Newsbeat* prints this, our visit could become part of the story, and there's no controlling what this woman might say about it."

"At least let's run a check on her through the Internet," Heather suggested. "With any luck, she's a nut case or an activist, and we can use that to discredit her. Any way we look at it, what she did was shitty."

Clarence nodded his agreement.

"What about this Madison Williams? Any idea who or where she is?"

Clarence thought of Lauren's warning. "We have to tread carefully here, too. If *Newsbeat* is looking for her and we start making noises about finding her, it's bound to get out. Then we are fucked. We give *Newsbeat* the smoking gun."

Tom, who had been standing by the window, turned. "What if we find her but hide her? At least until the convention."

Heather frowned. "Then what? If we hide her, it's gotta be permanent. This story would have just as much impact if not more in the lead-up to the primaries, too."

Clarence could sense the frustration rising in the room. They could all see their hard work going out of the window because of infidelity. The irony was that this time the infidelity was on the wife's part.

"What if we just let it ride and see what happens?" John raised his hand in defense as the others began to attack that suggestion. "No, hear me out. This could be good for Matt. Get him some sympathy votes."

"Hang Lauren out to dry?" Heather asked.

"Well, he didn't do anything wrong. He's the victim here."

Clarence thought it over as he looked out at the city. The buildings looked like distant shadows in the fog.

"You know the first rule," John told Clarence. "Get it out and live with it, then hope you can find something on McLennan that is worse."

"Do we know it's McLennan who's behind this?"

"Who else?" John replied. Matt's opponent for leadership of the Democratic Party had made it no secret that he would stop at nothing to get the nomination.

"Who would have thought that Lauren was gay? Jesus, that's fucked." John shook his head again.

Clarence frowned. "She's not. And I never want to hear those words again."

"Should we see what Matt wants to do?"

Clarence stood up and regarded the team. They were all dedicated to Matt, less because of his message than for the simple reason that they believed they were betting on a winning horse.

"I think what we need to do first is to buy some time. What do we have? One off-the-record source. Any top-flight newsmagazine will require a higher standard of proof—something like beyond a reasonable doubt, before it effectively decides the most critical primary election in recent memory. Or else it's one more step toward flushing our run at presidential politics down the toilet."

They all nodded. All of them had moved past shock, Clarence thought; their discussion was both feeling and practical. "Then maybe we do need to find the proof and eradicate it before anyone else does."

Clarence and Tom exchanged glances. Clarence nodded once. Tom moved from his post by the window. "Well, we've got work to do then."

Chapter
Eleven

Matt was tired. It had been one of those mornings, ever more frequent now, when his bones ached and a kind of sickening fatigue seized his entire body. His right hand was scratched and swollen from the grasping of a thousand well-wishing hands. And the bombshell Lauren had dropped the day before was still reverberating inside of him. Still, he was honest enough to understand that the shock he felt had more to do with the impact it would have on his chances than the very real betrayal by his wife. That reality had not yet sunk in. *Lauren and a woman?* The thought just floored him, and he refused to go there.

"I can't believe she would do this, now of all times." Matt started to pace as Clarence watched him. He was unwilling to contemplate the idea that he could not fix this. He shoved a hand through his hair and resumed his pacing. "She just expects that she can talk of our marriage ending and I won't have something to say about it." He turned around and looked at Clarence, who remained silent as he himself thought about the implications of Lauren leaving. "It won't happen, Clarence. I won't let it. She will be with me on this campaign if I have to personally drag her along. I don't care if she slept with half of Washington; my run to the White House will include my wife. She owes me that."

Clarence had his own doubts that Lauren would continue to go along with it all, but he didn't voice them. "You're about to be a candidate for the president of the USA. The reporters who follow you around are trained observers, at the top of their game, out of their minds half the time, with too fucking little to think about. Lauren's absence will start them asking questions, then it's only a small step to the discovery of the affair. And that's if someone else doesn't break it first, before we can stop it."

Something in Clarence's calm acceptance led Matt to a thought he hadn't had until then. "You knew, didn't you?"

If Clarence had a weakness, it was his discomfort with confronting Matt concerning personal matters. Clarence had that look now—narrow-eyed and pained, like a man with an unaccustomed hangover. His bulky form slumped in the chair.

Matt watched his friend of twenty years with disbelief. "How long have you been hiding this from me? What if it had come out before?"

"It was over two years ago, Matt. I didn't believe that anyone knew. It never occurred to me that Lauren would be spilling her guts to a shrink with a hard-on for Republicans." Clarence stared at his friend trying to read in the expressionless face where his thoughts were going. "How many things are *you* hiding? Things that no one, including Lauren, knows about?" The last part was his subtle reminder that Matt had just as many skeletons in his closet that could come out and play.

A complex mix of emotions—hurt, rage, and sheer appalled astonishment at his friend's presumption—overcame Matt. "Why the lies? What else are you keeping from me? You can't trust me on my own, is that it? I'm not quite up to the job without you to sell my soul for me?"

Circling his desk, Matt stood over his aide. "Who the hell do you think you are, or I am? What kind of president can I be? If I decide that being president requires a deal with the devil, I'll make it on my own. I've earned that right, God damn it. I'm running for president. Me, not you."

Clarence's eyes flickered as he fought down his own frustration. "It was an error in judgment, but at the time I believed it was the best decision."

"Best for whom, Clarence? Am I a puppet now? Someone you can pull and push and maneuver into the White House?"

"Matt, I will resign right this second if you can look me in the eye and say that knowing about the affair would have stopped you from running, would have made any difference at all."

Matt was buffeted by his deep loyalty to this man who had helped him through his entire career, and the flash of annoyed insight that, as always, Clarence was right. His ambition was stronger than any relationship he had. He would have buried it two years ago, too. They stared at each other, both irrevocably changed by the knowledge that they would stop at nothing to gain

the presidency. It was a sobering moment, scary in its implications. "You'll resign when I tell you to." Matt crossed back to this
desk. "We need to find out who leaked this document. Let's concentrate on McLennan's camp. They have the most to gain if this
comes out."

Clarence scratched his right ear as he pondered Matt's statement.

"Distract us and the press with the stories of your wife's affair?"
Matt nodded. "The reality is, if that is the type of game we are
engaged in this long before the Democratic Convention, they are
running scared." Clarence stood and looked at his friend for a
moment.

"The real question is, what does McLennan have to hide?"
Matt asked.

"Be careful, Matt. We might be able to survive Lauren's indis-
cretion, but if we start playing dirty, some other shit might come
out that could be more damaging to you personally." His pointed
look conveyed his meaning.

Matt gazed calmly back at him, then grabbed his mail from
the top of his desk. "Just find the dirt on McLennan. When you
do, I'll decide whether or not to use it. And *I'll* take care of Lauren."

The tall, long-legged redhead was rinsing glasses when she
glanced toward the front door as it opened. She frowned when she
recognized the woman in the doorway.

"Hi, Darcy."

"What do you want?" Her tone was uncharacteristically
unfriendly, but she remembered only too well how devastated
Madison had been and could not find it in herself to be nice.

Lauren crossed to the bar. "Tea would be nice."

Darcy stared at her, trying to intimidate her into leaving,
though Lauren appeared almost amused at the transparent
attempt. "There's a coffee shop at the corner," she finally said.

"Yeah? Well, I'm here now. You can make it to go, if that will
help." Lauren's tone was wry.

Darcy almost smiled at that, then caught herself and assumed
a fierce look. She did not want to like this woman at all. She
crossed to the coffee bar and prepared the tea in a paper cup and
placed it in front of Lauren. The fact that it was a to-go cup was

not lost on Lauren. Darcy crossed her arms, the better to glower at her.

Ignoring the glare, Lauren took the cup and gently blew on it. "Got milk?"

After a pause, Darcy sighed heavily and reluctantly placed a small jug of milk and a bowl of sugar in front of her and resumed her deliberate glare.

"You don't like me much, do you?" Lauren finally asked as the silence stretched between them.

"Not much."

"I need to get in touch with Madison. Do you know where she is?"

Darcy's laugh was short. "Forget it."

"Darcy, it's important."

"Yeah? Still married, I hear."

Lauren hid her hurt at the accuracy of the jab. "Darcy, I need to warn her of something. Please."

They stared at each other. Darcy was the first to look away. "What do you want with her? Haven't you done enough damage?"

Lauren's gaze was steady. She refused to show that the words stung as they hit close to home. She had lived with enough recrimination and guilt over the years that the thick skin she had developed allowed her to not let the accusation shatter her. "It took two people, Darcy. I wasn't the only one involved in all of it."

"Yeah? You were the only one married and still sleeping with your husband, though."

Suddenly unbearably tired, Lauren rubbed her eyes. "Darcy, fun as this is, I don't have the energy to go a round with you today. Can I take a rain check on getting insulted until another day?"

Darcy's opened her mouth to retort, but something in Lauren's eyes stopped her. She noticed the sadness that seemed to be permanently buried there, and felt a tug of concern. She was not a naturally mean person, and seeing someone so obviously hurting gave her pause, no matter how hard she was trying to dislike her. She grabbed a piece of paper and wrote something down and handed it to Lauren.

"What's this?"

Darcy smirked. "A rain check."

Lauren had to smile. "Gee, thanks."

"Want something stronger than tea?"

Lauren's look was amused. "Like arsenic?"

Darcy's mouth twitched in response. "Something a bit stronger."

Lauren held the barkeep's eyes for a moment, trying to gauge where she was coming from. She seemed satisfied, for she nodded. "Sure."

Keith had gone through every phone book of every decent-sized city in the state of Massachusetts. Still no sign of any Madison Williams. If she was a doctor, she wasn't practicing there. He straightened, and felt the kinks in his back protest. Just as he was thinking of grabbing a beer and a sandwich at the deli on the corner, his cell phone went off. "McGraw."

"I think I found her."

Keith stopped and quickly looked around, then caught himself in the act of automatically checking for eavesdroppers. *I'm getting paranoid,* he thought with a grim smile. "Shoot." He grabbed his ever-present pad and paper, cradling the cell phone between his shoulder and his neck.

"It appears there *was* a Dr. Madison Williams at St. Mary's, and she *did* leave two years ago. It fact, it looks like she resigned to teach."

"Teach? You mean teach as in a school?"

"Yeah. But that's not all. It looks like she is now teaching at Boston U."

"She's in Boston?"

"Looks like." The voice was smug.

"Any forwarding address?"

"I'll need a few more hours for that."

Keith wrote out what he knew, then hung up. He was always amazed at what they could find, given the time. It was just a matter of digging. Sometimes he believed that reporters were better at finding out stuff than cops ever could be. He smiled at that, and decided that a beer was definitely in order.

"Good God! What happened?" Madison jumped up in concern as Jamie walked into Darcy's café, her left eye swollen shut. The bruising around the eye was a wild mixture of color. Jamie, a homicide detective like Alex, had been partnered with a rookie that week, and it was not going well. Years of working with Alex had built a cohesive unit, instinctively in tune with each other. Breaking in a new partner had proven to be a difficult and painful task for Jamie, who had little tolerance for mistakes. The fact that she now had made a mistake a rookie would make was especially galling to her.

Jamie made a face as she sat down. "Some punk decided to resist arrest. He managed one good swing." She didn't want to talk about it, still too steamed to be even remotely amused. To top off her foul mood, her head throbbed, despite the handful of painkillers she had swallowed an hour earlier. Madison knelt beside her, her fingers gently lifting her face as she examined the injury. Jamie blew out an impatient breath at the unspoken concern. "Maddie, I'm fine."

Madison ignored her as her cool, practiced fingers gently probed the area, making Jamie wince.

"Ouch."

"Do you have a headache?"

"No," Jamie lied. Madison watched her critically for a moment, and Jamie squirmed under the attention. "Doc, I've already been to emergency."

"Okay."

Darcy, who had been in the back of the restaurant, sauntered back in and made her way to the table. She took a step back as she saw Jamie's face. "Wow, champ, what does the other guy look like?"

"Worse. Get me a beer, will ya? I'm still pissed."

Darcy grinned. "My hero." She left to get the order. The café was not yet open, allowing them the chance to enjoy a few hours together without being disturbed.

Madison looked at Jamie. "Want to talk about it?"

Jamie made a face, forgetting about the bruises, then winced as her facial muscles screamed in protest. "Damn. Ouch! No. It will only get me steamed." She blew out a breath. "I let my guard down for one minute; it was a stupid mistake a rookie would have made. My pride hurts more than my eye. The guys have been riding me since it happened." It still annoyed her to know that for one brief moment, someone had been able to slip under her guard. "I would sooner talk about something else." She changed the subject with a smile. "So, how are you? Any cute students in your class worth a little police attention?"

Darcy, who had returned with their drinks, sat down and

smirked at Jamie. "What do you want to do, scare them?"

"Funny." Having only one eye to glare at her hostess diminished its effectiveness, so Jamie chose to ignore her instead.

"I have an announcement to make," Madison said after a beat. Two sets of eyes looked at her with interest. "I've decided to start dating again." She waited for their reaction. It was minimal, as they continued to merely look at her. "Did you hear what I just said?"

"Yeah. You said you're ready to date again," Jamie repeated calmly. Darcy just sat drinking.

"That's it? After all of the harassment I've gotten from you two about this, that's all the reaction I'm getting?"

The two women looked at one another. "How many times does this make?" Jamie asked. "Three?"

"No, I think this is the fourth time."

Madison made a face at them. "Yeah, yeah. I mean it this time."

"Like you meant it six months ago when I arranged for you to meet my friend Cindy?" Darcy asked.

"Oh, I like Cindy; she is nice," Jamie contributed helpfully.

"She *is* great," Darcy agreed. "So, poor Cindy asked me the next day what was wrong with my good friend, Madison. The entire date, grunts and monosyllables were all she got in her attempts at striking up a conversation with the doc here. I told her you had a speech impediment." Darcy started to laugh at that.

"What?" Madison frowned, taking exception.

"I didn't want her to take it personally."

Madison shrugged. "I wasn't quite ready then, but I am now." A raised eyebrow was the only response. "I need to have sex, you guys," Madison admitted softly.

"Oh, well, that's different." Jamie smiled. "I'll gladly help you with that little issue myself. I mean, what are friends for?" At the look on Madison's face, she started to laugh. "Oh, honey, don't ever change. I'm kidding. Jesus, you look petrified. Being with me is not that frightening a prospect. Women usually beg me to be with them."

"With that shiner, champ, you would scare a blind person," Darcy teased.

"You only wish you could get this body."

"Get it for what? Are you so desperate that you're offering it to all your friends now?"

Madison watched them with affection. *God, I love those two.*
"Guys? Hello?" She raised her voice as they continued their gentle
bantering. "I'd like to get back to me and my problem."

"What problem?"

Madison sighed exasperated. "The fact that I would like to
have sex sometime this century."

Darcy turned to her. "Honey, there's a difference between
dating somebody and picking someone up for a good fuck. A good
fuck usually doesn't require much conversation."

Jamie stared at her in amazement. "You are so crude. I'm
amazed at what comes out of your mouth sometimes."

"Why? Am I not right?"

"Yes...but there are ways of expressing it."

"I just did. You're not that delicate. Why beat around the
bush? You both totally got what I was talking about, didn't you?"

Jamie shook her head with a smile, then turned to Madison.
"What my crude friend was trying to say is that if all you want to
do is have sex, you don't need to start dating. There are such
things as one-night stands."

"I know. But seriously, I'm ready to meet someone. It's been
long enough."

Darcy jumped up. "Well, if you mean it, this calls for a cele-
bration." She left and soon after they heard the quiet pop of a
champagne cork, then she returned with a bottle and three glasses.
"Here's to us finding a sex life." A sentiment which they all
toasted.

Chapter Twelve

The flight attendant took the boarding pass with a practiced robotic smile. "Welcome aboard; third row, left side." Her eyes caught Lauren's and held them for a minute longer than necessary. The look was one of acknowledgement and interest, but Lauren's answering smile was distracted. Lauren sat down and toyed with the belt buckle. She was edgy, and knew she was on the verge of losing whatever control she held over her emotions. She could hardly believe that she was actually doing this. She was possibly hours away from being face to face with the woman that she had loved beyond reason a couple of years before; and without knowing what the outcome of the meeting would be, she sensed that her feelings had not diminished with time.

This trip was impulsive; she hadn't thought any further than booking a hotel room and getting on a plane. She knew that, regardless of what happened next, she was embarking on a path of no return. Whether or not the story came out now was irrelevant. She had been forced to confront her feelings about where she was finding herself at this point in her life, and the direction she didn't want to take. For two years she had been going through the motions, not allowing herself to feel anything. In the beginning, she had wanted and missed Madison with a ferocity that stunned her. She needed only to recall some fleeting image and she would be overwhelmed by desire, and the need to touch, to taste, to lose herself in her lover.

Despite the pain those thoughts brought, she had welcomed those moments because it was only their presence that convinced her that some part of her still lived. But with the passing of months and years, she started moving though her days—numb, barely present. Existing by going through the motions of living.

This protective numbness had quickly been destroyed by the confrontation with Keith, and the hardest part had been facing Matt and admitting to the affair. As she sat beside him, it had become so clear that she had never been in love with him, didn't love him enough to go on pretending. In the emotional wake of her admission, she was left with the feeling that she couldn't go on with the charade she was being asked to participate in; she no longer had an excuse to do so. Reluctant to leave him and unwilling to hurt him, she had been so afraid of taking a chance on the unknown that she had given up her own chance at happiness two years before. She still had those feelings, but now they were less about leaving him and more about herself.

She was fed up with not being happy. To be this close to discovery was almost a relief. It was forcing her to acknowledge that she had never been happier than when she was with Madison, and that even if her former lover was no longer in the picture, loving Madison had taught her that she had only loved with such deep passion because Madison was a woman. That realization had come late to her, but finally dawned as she sat there beside the man she had lived with, but never deeply loved. Waking up one morning in the White House would be a disaster, and she could not live with that possibility any longer.

She probably didn't deserve another shot at her relationship with Madison, but she had discovered a resolve to at least come clean with her past, to live in truth. Hence this impromptu trip. She sighed as she looked out of the window. The ache for Madison was still there under the surface, like an itch impossible to get at.

"Well, well, well. Fancy meeting you on this flight, Lauren. What a coincidence." Keith couldn't believe his good fortune.

His voice broke through her concentration, and she felt her heart stutter at the unwelcome interruption. *Coincidence is another word for rotten luck.* She turned to Keith with a smile that stopped short of her eyes. "Hello, Keith."

He sat uninvited beside her. "Do you fly to Boston much these days?"

"No."

As she turned away from him, he asked, "Mind my asking what you are doing in Boston?" His tone was almost smug.

"Yes, I mind."

Keith stood up as the flight attendant asked him to take his seat. "Wouldn't have anything to do with Dr. Madison Williams living in Boston, would it?"

She looked at him and smiled sweetly. "Fuck you, Keith." She leaned her head back and closed her eyes, effectively tuning him out.

They were restless. Friday afternoon was never a good time to start discussing the implications of prescribing the wrong drug. Madison could usually hold their attention, but something in the air today had them all fidgeting, herself included. She glanced at her watch and noted ruefully that there were still forty-five minutes left in the session. *To hell with it.* She glanced at the class, and with an amused shake of her head she said, "Okay, I get it; we all have the fever, myself included. Why don't we call it a week?" She grinned at the startled yet hopeful looks. "Go on, before I change my mind." They left hurriedly as if afraid she would change her mind. If she were the sensitive sort, the haste with which they had departed would have left her uncertain of her capabilities as a teacher. Chuckling, she erased the board.

Back in her office, she started listening to her voice mail. One message stopped her cold and she sank down onto a chair, her legs no longer able to support her. Even after two years, the voice had the power to shatter her heart into a thousand small pieces. Intent on the urgency in the voice, she was replaying the message when the phone rang again. She stared at it, heart racing, then picked up the receiver gingerly. "Madison Williams."

"Madison? It's Darcy."

Madison grinned at the phone, relief flooding through her. "Hey there. Still pining away for me?" Instead of the usual banter, the silence from Darcy was telling. "What's wrong?"

"Something strange happened today. It could mean nothing, but some reporter called and started asking about you. He knew you'd lived here once, I guess, and wanted to know where you were now."

Madison frowned, puzzled as to why a reporter would be looking for her. "Did he say why he was looking for me?"

"That's just it, Madison—he wanted to ask you about Lauren. He asked if I remembered her being around a couple of years ago."

Madison stared sightlessly into the room. *So that's why she called.*

"I told him I didn't know where you were, and though I recognized Lauren's name from the TV, I didn't remember ever seeing her around. I don't know if he believed me or not, but he left me his number in case I should remember anything else. I hope I did the right thing." Her voice reflected her uncertainty. She was about to mention Lauren's visit, but something stopped her. If Lauren did not contact Madison, then the visit was unimportant. She did not want to be responsible for reopening wounds.

"Yeah, you did."

"What's going on?"

"I don't know. Do me a favor: if anyone else comes looking for me, let me know. Don't tell them anything." She stared at the phone, feeling her heart pound. *Why would anyone try to contact me regarding Lauren?* Well, there was one way to find out, if she was brave enough.

Halfway into the flight, Lauren focused on the very real problem of Keith being on the same plane. She had no doubt that he would try to follow her, find out where she was going. Her mind swirled, trying to figure out a way to escape him. As they taxied, Lauren grabbed hold of her jacket and stretched her legs. Keith was several rows back in economy, so she would have a slight time advantage. Thankfully, Logan Airport was not that large and the flight attendant had given her clear directions to the hotel, which was connected to the airport through a different terminal. As soon as they reached the gate and had come to a stop, she was the first through the doors. She hoped that the attendant would run some interference for her. Even a few minutes would help.

Keith shoved his way to the front of the queue of deplaning passengers and ran down the set of stairs. By the time he made it out to the terminal, Lauren was gone. He jogged to the area where the rental car counters were and saw no sign of her, then dashed outside to scan the pick-up area for limousines and taxis. Several cars were waiting, but again he saw no sign of Lauren. He shook his head in frustration and released a deep breath. At least he had Madison's address, and if Lauren was going anywhere near there, he would find her. He marched back to the rental counter with a satisfied nod. The chase was on.

There was a soft tap on the door, then another. Inside the

hotel room, Lauren stopped pacing. Pausing for an instant to prepare herself, she went to answer.

Madison stood in the doorway. As the door opened wider, her eyes lifted and met Lauren's. Their eyes engaged for only a second or two, but if the exchange had lasted an eternity it wouldn't have been more meaningful. In a flash, the years fell away.

"Hello."

"Hello back."

Lauren's eyes took her in. She stood in the artificial light, dressed in jeans and a sweater. Her hair, a little longer now, fell in a tumble of waves to her shoulders. It had been almost two years. Madison looked older to Lauren; more beautiful than ever, but tempered by experience. There was tension around that wonderful mouth, a wary look in her eyes, but she looked so good that for a moment Lauren wanted to go to her. Instead, she stepped back and motioned for Madison to enter. They smiled, and then they stopped smiling and just looked at each other. "You look wonderful. I'm glad you came," Lauren said quietly.

That's all it took for all of Madison's efforts to get over her lost love to shatter, to come to nothing. Just like that, Madison felt her heart tumble. She looked away, unable to deal with gazing at Lauren again. "Your message said it was urgent."

"Sit, please. I need to tell you something." Lauren tried to find a way to start. Telling Madison about Keith's visit—the therapist's notes, Keith's question, her lie in return—she watched Madison closely. Madison's stillness was so complete that she seemed not to breathe. Whatever Lauren had expected, it was not this. Except for the look in her eyes, Madison could have been thinking of anything—a terrible regret, the fear of discovery, but the raw feelings were evident and almost painful to see.

"Are *you* okay?" she asked Lauren.

"Not really. I feel devastated and numb at the same time. Because of then, and because of now."

Madison stood up. "Does Matt know?"

"Yes."

"I'm sorry; that must have been difficult."

Lauren glanced at Madison, looking for signs of disappointment in her inability to confront anything painful. There were none, only blank shock and sadness. Seeing her here in her hotel room was almost more than Lauren could stand. "I've imagined seeing you again," Lauren finally said. "A thousand ways. In my heart, it was always as if the last two years had never happened. That somehow, we'd still be us...But I never expected that I would love you still...that I would be in love with you still..."

Stunned because Lauren's admission reflected so many of her own feelings, Madison closed her eyes. How many times had she wished she could have the last days of their affair to live again, the chance to choose some other path? But now she felt diminished, trapped by the harsh reality of the decisions she had made two years before. Tears welled in her eyes.

"Did you ever think of me? Of our meeting again?" Lauren asked quietly.

Madison sighed, unwilling to go there. "Lauren..."

"Talk to me, Madison. Tell me what you're thinking. "

She looked at Lauren, older now, wearier, but still so emotionally immediate; so much the same incredible woman she had loved that at first the recognition overwhelmed her. She shook her head. "No, I can't," she managed.

"Why not?"

Madison turned to her. "Aside from all the guilt and regret? Yours and mine?"

"Don't you think—" Lauren started but, torn between anger and despair, Madison interrupted her.

"Lauren, what is this?" She turned away, fighting the emotional roller coaster of emotions that had been triggered the minute she had heard her former lover's voice on her answering machine. "What do you want from me? What do you want me to say? You tell me the press is about to out us in more ways than I could have imagined. You are still married, and the last time I checked, your husband was running for higher office. Do you want me to tell you that I still want you? What can come of it? We can't sneak around again. And once we're out of the closet, the vultures will pick our bones. When did our affair start? Tonight?" Her heart bleeding, her voice tried to reason. "It would be all they need. Any way you look at it, people still get hurt."

Lauren thrust her hands into her pockets. Her response was etched with frustration. "That's what we said two years ago. Look how well it's worked."

Madison gazed at her steadily. "Then let's have the rest of the conversation. Two years ago you told me that you were afraid of hurting Matt and his chances to be president. You didn't know how to leave him. What has changed? You are still with him."

She didn't bring up the pregnancy, but it was there between them, the pain of their parting unacknowledged.

Lauren shook her head, tears in her eyes. "I admit I didn't handle it well. I just needed time. A chance. I was trying to deal not only with the knowledge that I needed to end my marriage, but also trying to come to understand what being gay might mean to my career, my life. To change my life so completely and so quickly was terrifying. Now I am just looking for a solution that we can all live with. It's only a matter of time. What if I do what I need to do, then can we start dating? No one needs to know that we talk every night. I have missed that. I have missed you."

Madison felt the sweetness and the ache of the words pull at her, and she closed her eyes against the onslaught of emotion. Heartsick, she slowly shook her head. "I have missed that, too, but, Lauren, it's not up to me. And they won't give us a chance. Unless you can figure something out quickly, you will hurt your husband and possibly destroy any chance of his ever being president. And then we are back to where we were two years ago, having the same conversation. I can't sneak around again. I won't. Not even for you. Why do you always try to make *me* see the truth? Why can't *you* for once?" *Why couldn't you just leave him?* she wanted to say, but didn't.

The quiet words seemed to pierce Lauren. "I did see the truth. Two years ago. When I begged you not to go. I told you then that I wanted to be with you, but you weren't ready to listen."

Madison looked away. "Sometimes I wish I had," she said at last. "Sometimes I wish I could have lived with giving you an ultimatum, but I believed that for us to work you needed to arrive at your own truth without a gun being held to your head. And you're wrong... I did wait for you."

Alex had had to physically restrain her after she found out about the miscarriage. It had devastated her not to be there, and she had flown back to New York to try to find out how Lauren was. She had roamed the hospital corridors until Matt left, then stood outside the door, about to go in when Clarence had stopped her. He had made her see that she didn't belong there. But she kept waiting for Lauren to call.

And she wouldn't tell Lauren how devastated she had felt watching a newscast one night, months later, to know that Lauren was still with Matt and they were gearing up for a run for the

White House. Her heart had broken again. She had resigned from the hospital the next day, and after a few months, had started teaching. Alex and Darcy had been her lifelines as she tried to put the pieces of her life back together again. Only in the last six months had she felt like she had moved on, and now it was as if no time had passed. Here they were, with Lauren asking if there was any chance for them to be together. And so many impediments still in their way... She shook her head ruefully. "Please, let's stop this. Before we do more damage."

Lauren crossed to her, touched her face gently. The feel of her hand was a sweet ache that weakened Madison's resolve. "Tell me one thing then?"

Madison looked into golden eyes. "What is it?"

"Do you still love me?" Lauren asked.

Despite herself, Madison felt the tears well again. "Oh, Lauren, that's such a sad question."

"Why?"

For a moment, Madison considered telling the truth. She had lived alone all her adult life, so when she was by herself at home she was never afraid. Loneliness was more frightening to her than the threat of an intruder. She didn't feel the need to protect herself from burglars, but she steeled herself against the emptiness she felt on holidays, when even the company of good friends didn't compensate for the lack of a family. Solitude didn't make for coziness, even when sitting in front of a fireplace on a cold night. When she was startled awake in the middle of the night, it wasn't because of imagined noises, but because of the all-too-real silence of living alone. The only fear she had of being by herself was that she would be by herself for the rest of her life.

If ever there had been someone who had a chance of touching her—her mind, her heart, the spot in her spirit where Madison really lodged—it had been Lauren. She had been the one allowed to relieve the solitude, fill the emptiness, banish the silence, and share her life. But romantic notions were a luxury she couldn't afford. Not now. Not after all that had happened. Too much had happened for her to be able to recapture the moment. And she was sad for it. And then she found a second, easier truth. Softly she said, "Because the answer doesn't matter."

Later that night in the stairwell of a Boston office building,

Keith took cover from the rain. He had so far been unsuccessful in finding Madison at the university. He was now waiting a few doors away from the address he had been given, speaking into his cellular phone. "Did you get to the therapist?"

"We did. She confirmed that Taylor was a patient, that Taylor met with her in confidence, that Taylor talked about the affair. According to her, the senator's wife was devastated."

"Yeah, that's pretty clear from the notes."

"The problem is the therapist won't talk on the record. She is claiming the notes were stolen; I think she feels guilty about talking."

"Why shouldn't she? I mean, violating Lauren's right to privacy is one thing, but ruining her life should give this lady a little pause."

"You still don't like this, do you?"

"'Don't like' is too mild."

"Well, forget all that. Stop worrying about Lauren Taylor. Nobody made her sleep with a woman."

"I never said my feelings were important, just that I have them." Keith swallowed his distaste. "You know the thing that has been bugging me is how we got the therapist's notes. If this does pan out, who would have the most to gain?"

"Who the fuck cares? I don't care how or why we got it, only whether or not we can prove it. You might try Lauren again. If she's not talking, go to the husband. And find that Williams woman."

Madison drove home, Madonna blasting from the speakers. Anything to block out the thoughts, images, awakening needs that were crowding in on all sides. Seeing Lauren again had been a mistake. All the feelings had come back, flooding through her in an unstoppable tide. As she turned onto her street, she fought off the urge to bang her head against the steering wheel in frustration. Nearing her tidy brownstone, she saw the silhouette of a man huddled in the shared driveway, talking on a cell phone. She slowed, trying to see if she recognized him. He hung up and crouched back against the side of the building; and Madison suddenly felt his stare across the street, the recognition in his eyes. Or was she imagining things?

She drove past her house, her teeth worrying her bottom lip.

Without knowing how she knew, she instinctively realized that the man was waiting for her. She pressed down on the gas pedal, eyes locked to her rearview mirror trying to see if he was following her. Half chiding herself for paranoia, she grabbed for her cell phone and pressed a number. "Alex? Listen, I need to stay with you tonight. I'll explain later." She threw the phone next to her on the seat and turned west, throwing worried glances behind her. Which was ridiculous, since she didn't know what kind of car he drove, or if in fact he was even after her.

"Not that I'm not delighted to see you, but what gives?" Alex asked as she and Madison sat at the kitchen table sharing a coffee.

"I saw Lauren tonight."

Alex stared at her. "What? *Our* Lauren? Lauren *Taylor?*"

"Yeah. Lauren."

"Jesus, why would you do that?" Alex erupted, memory of Madison's near breakdown still fresh in her mind.

"She called."

"Oh, well...that makes it all right, then," she replied sarcastically.

Madison had to smile at the fierce frown. "Is that your scary cop face?"

"Maddie..." Alex tried, exasperated.

"Alex... *Anyways,* she called because she wanted to warn me about a reporter who is sniffing around about us and what happened. It seems that he got hold of notes from a therapy session that Lauren attended when she and I broke up..." She paused. "I guess breaking up is not the right term, since technically we weren't really going out."

In frustration, Alex slapped a hand down on the table. "Madison, why didn't she just tell you that over the phone? Did she really need to tell you in person?"

That stopped Madison. She didn't really have an answer for that. Her confusion showed on her face. *Why* had *Lauren...*

Alex shook her head as she read the puzzlement. "Maddie..."

"What?" Pulled from her musings, she spoke in a defensive tone.

"Do you really want to go there again?"

"Where? I'm not anywhere. I saw her, we talked, she warned me, and that's that."

"I see. Is that why you are shaking?"

"I'm not shak—" Alex grabbed her hand and lifted it. Madison noticed the trembling in her fingers. "Well, I have a reporter chasing after me; anyone would be upset."

Alex was unconvinced. "Mm-hmm. Okay, so you saw her and you talked, and then you're driving home, and decided you wanted to stay here instead?"

"There you go again, acting like a cop."

"I am a cop."

Madison made a face. "I think there's a reporter waiting for me at my place, probably the same man who was questioning Lauren. He was hiding in my driveway."

"What?" Alex jumped up in full protective mode. "What does he look like?"

"I don't know." She shrugged. "Male."

Alex rolled her eyes. "Civilians." She marched to the phone and made a call. "Tim? Ryan here. Listen, I need you to send a car over to 1022 Charter Road. There's a report of a man lurking there—probably in a car, maybe sniffing around the driveway. Can you make him disappear?" She listened to his reply. "I don't care. Charge him with trespassing, loitering, and illegal parking in a snow removal zone. I know it's not snowing, just do it. His description?" Her eyes met Madison's and she grinned. "Male." With a satisfied smile, she replaced the receiver, cutting off his eruption. "That takes care of that. Back to you, now. How was it, seeing Lauren again?"

Madison avoided the startling blue eyes. "How is it that we've known each other all these years, and I've never noticed how pushy you are?"

"Don't change the subject."

Madison sighed. "What do you think?"

"I think one of the things seeing her again did was to scare you, so you came here to hide."

"I'm not scared."

Alex raised a skeptical eyebrow. "No?"

"No. I'm terrified." Madison stood up, unable to be still. "I stood in front of her, and it was as if I had seen her only yesterday. And all I could think about was how good it was to see her, to stand there next to her. Two years of trying to forget her, and one look and I'm nowhere."

Alex looked at her friend thoughtfully. "Honey, did you really expect it to be different?"

"Yes...no...don't know." Madison pushed an impatient hand through her dark hair. "I just thought that maybe I had imagined how good it was. With time, the mind does funny things. It just remembers all the great things and forgets the rest. I thought, 'I'm going to see her and I'll realize how unattractive she really is, and it will help me with closure.' Stuff like that."

"And?"

"It helped me, all right. Shit." Her eyes filled with tears. "God damn it to hell!"

Heart breaking for her friend, Alex pulled Madison into her arms. "I'm sorry you hurt. I'm sorry for the both of you. You are both great, and you deserve so much more."

Madison impatiently rubbed the wetness from her cheeks. "She looked at me and something just settled over me, like it always did around her. It's like a feeling that this is where I belong. And she is still married, and he's running for the damn presidency, and I'm sick to death of feeling like walking away from what we had was the wrong thing to do."

Clarence looked up from the folder he was studying. "Who else has seen this?"

Tom Reynolds shrugged. "Just me and my investigator."

Clarence threw it on his desk. "Jesus. When it rains it pours, doesn't it? I guess now we are going to see who has the biggest balls." He stood up, his way of saying the meeting was over. "Leave it with me." Clarence watched Tom leave, then turned to the folder and reread the police report and the sealed investigation. He had a feeling that they were all standing on the edge of a precipice, and they were all either going to jump or be pushed off. There was no way of knowing who would survive. He shook his head and picked up the telephone.

Clarence watched Matt read the file.

"Well, I'll be damned. I never took McLennan for a wife beater," he said, looking up. "How did you get this?"

Clarence looked pained. "I'd rather not say. The less you know..."

Matt dismissed that with an impatient wave of his hand. "Do

you know if he did it again? Or where the files are now?"

"About the files, they're in storage. McLennan had them sealed." Clarence's tone was even. "If McLennan's guilty of domestic violence, even once, he's a dead man. Or at least severely wounded." Clarence paused for a moment. "If McLennan's the one who fed the Lauren story to *Newsbeat,* this incident alone should be enough to keep him from giving it to anyone else. Assuming it's still under their control, the McLennan people will make a deal."

"*If* it was McLennan," Matt retorted. "But we don't know that."

"Who else?" Clarence's tone was emphatic. "If McLennan beat his wife, even once, does it matter who leaked Lauren's story? It won't matter to the press."

Matt stared at him. "It matters to me."

"But why should it? The result's the same—he looks worse than you and Lauren do." Clarence's tone was soft again. "I know you don't like this; neither do I, but I'm trying to be practical. You don't deserve to lose because of Lauren. The country deserves better than McClennan, too."

Torn between his ambition and his honor, Matt turned from his friend. As a kid he had always thought that running for office was a noble thing, a great thing to strive for. That belief had disappeared the minute he had run for Congress. What was it about the ambition to be president that destroyed all values and sense of moral decency in anyone involved in the running? Winning at all costs: that was the name of the game. No one really understood the sacrifices the battle required until they got into the thick of it. He certainly hadn't.

When it came down to it, democracy had a funny way of choosing its leaders. The requirements included destroying anyone who stood in the way of his getting to the White House, paying off debts and collecting them, and selling out his friends for the same things he himself had done several times. Why didn't that leave a bitter taste in his mouth? Where was his sense of right and wrong?

There was an awareness in him now of a fundamental flaw in his character. He lacked a moral center—or at least his ambition obscured it at the best of times—making it difficult to decide whenever his integrity and ambition battled. In order to improve his chances of winning an election, he was sitting there in his

office discussing ways to destroy his opponent by using something
that had been done twenty years earlier. Just so he could be head
of state. He thought of Lauren and what he was asking her to do.
Should he feel guilty for asking her to sacrifice her life for the sake
of his ambition? He didn't have an answer for that. And that was
the thing that upset him the most. He should know what the right
thing to do was, but he didn't.

Chapter
Thirteen

Lauren was alone in the Georgetown house, stealing a few minutes of quiet with Matt busy at the office. Seeing Madison had clarified so much for her, to the point of absurdity. She knew that regardless of what did or didn't happen between them, she definitely would not stay with Matt. Guilt was a very strong motivator for inaction, but at last she was ready for the ending of their marriage. It had taken her years to get to that point, and only under threat of exposure was she able to ask herself the truly hard questions. But at least she had. She could no longer continue living the lie that was her life. Her mind was at peace with that decision.

She paced, trying to decide what to do next. She had sacrificed so much to support Matt's ambition. Her desire not to hurt him or his chances for the presidency was strong, and now, as before, she despaired of not achieving a resolution they could all live with. Then she stopped moving, frozen by a thought. She had always been a strong proponent of integrity in the news, and now the thought that crept in gave her pause. *Can I do this?* She was about to cross the line.

She turned to the kitchen counter and rifled through her phone book, searching for an entry. *Please be in. Please be in.* Fingers tapping nervously on the counter, she waited as the phone rang. "Stephen? Lauren Taylor." At the reply, she smiled. "Yeah, it has been a long time. I need to see you away from your office. It's urgent." She held her breath at the pause, then released it softly. "Yeah, I'll be there in twenty minutes." She replaced the receiver, knowing that she was about to engage in a battle between a reporter's desire to get at the truth and her own resolve to protect everyone she loved. More than that, selfishly, she was looking for a way to be with Madison.

She arrived at the residence of the editor in chief for *Newsbeat* and rang the bell. He greeted her at the door, a man in his fifties, still handsome despite his receding hairline. Dressed in cream cotton pants and a white T-shirt, his bare feet sinking into the thick carpet, he looked more like a yuppie professor than an aggressive editor. He motioned her in. "I was surprised by your call, Lauren," he said, his smile cool, his eyes watchful.

She studied him. Did he know what his reporters were working on? She returned his smile. "I'm just as surprised to be here, Stephen."

Theirs was a casual friendship. She hadn't seen him in a year or so. Hadn't spent any time with him really since the time when they had both gotten drunk in a hole in New Mexico, and he had spilled more than he should have. She had never brought it up, and he had been grateful. She was about to call him on it. "Stephen, I need a favor."

He raised one eyebrow. The bright blue eyes that seemed to catch everything stared back at her steadily, not hinting at what he thought of her unexpected appearance on his doorstep.

"One of your reporters has damaging information that could hurt my husband's chances."

His smile was sardonic. There it was. There always was something. "Is that right? Something he did?"

"No. Something I did."

"I keep a very long arm's length, Lauren. I don't tell my reporters how to report. Freedom of the press and all that."

"Stephen, your reporter is in possession of some confidential notes from a therapist I saw two years ago. Whether or not the notes were stolen will be of interest to the police, and there is enough there for a lawsuit. But that is not what I want to talk about." She took a deep breath, suddenly unnerved by confronting the truth. "The notes deal with an affair I had years ago."

"Oh?" There was amusement on his face.

She recognized it and prayed she still held the ace. "With a woman." She said it quietly, watching his eyes. That stopped him. Their eyes met, his wary, hers steady, conveying a message behind the soft words.

"Ha..." He stood up and walked over to the bar set into the cream-colored wall. He poured some Scotch into a couple of tumblers and added a splash of soda to one. He handed her one and raised his in a mock toast. "Here's to us lost souls."

She sipped hers, watching him over the rim of her glass. Years before, he had drunkenly admitted to being in love with a younger man. Married for twenty-six years, father of four, he took to seeing him on business trips. She had protected his privacy, and now she was collecting her marker.

Stephen rubbed his chin, his eyes still guarded. "You're giving me a hell of dilemma, Lauren. I never interfere. I can't very well call them up and tell them to stop pursuing the story. They'll scream 'freedom of the press' and 'censorship' until CNN picks up the story."

"I understand. I'm the press too, remember? I'm not asking you to kill the story, I'm asking you to delay it."

"Until?"

"Until after the convention."

"Who's my guy?"

"Keith McGraw."

He nodded. He turned to the bar once again. "Want another drink?"

"Sure." They took their drinks out on the balcony. The air was still, with the distant sound of traffic occasionally piercing the quiet.

"Does the senator know?"

"Yeah."

He looked at her admiringly. "Well, that took guts."

She dismissed it with a shrug. "Guts or no choice. Take your pick."

"Who is the woman?"

"Try another question, Stephen."

He smiled at her dry tone and lifted his glass in mock salute. "Touché." They drank in companionable silence. "What are you going to do?" he finally asked.

"I don't really know. What would you do if you were me?"

"Me? I'm a coward, too attached to my comforts to rock my world, so I would deny it, pretend it hadn't happened, and live unhappily ever after." He said it mockingly, but she heard the sadness behind the flippant tone.

"I've done that. For two years." She turned to him. "Stephen, do you think his candidacy could survive our separating?"

He looked at her in surprise. "Are you serious?"

"Afraid so. I'm tired of living a lie." She leaned against the railing, watching the blinking lights in the distance. "This wasn't just a fling or an itch I needed to scratch; this was it for me. Two years later I'm still having the same damn conversation, and I'm finally too exhausted by that to keep going in the same direction."

He looked thoughtful, seriously considering her plight. "Then I would deny it when it came out."

"You mean lie? I can't do that. I'm leaving Matt precisely because I can't lie to him or to myself anymore."

"Lie. Look, Lauren, the minute you get to Washington is the minute the truth disappears. Matt knows that better than anyone else. The trick is not to get caught at it. So, deny it. Threaten to sue us, whatever. Ride out the storm, then once he's in, announce a separation. By then, hope something else is on the front pages. There usually is." He smiled at her. "And keep away from her. Or else your lies mean squat."

"Ah...well, that is the dilemma." She finished her drink, felt the glow of the Scotch warm her. "Where did our standards go, Stephen? We used to be able to tell the difference between journalism and show biz, between truth and dishonesty. When did we sink knee deep in the muck?"

"The minute the story became a 30-second clip," he replied with a smile that held no humor. "Catch their attention with the headlines; win the ratings at all cost; get the Emmy: all in 30 seconds. That's when all of us so-called serious journalists forgot about ethics, about privacy, about chasing after a story only if it was worth telling. We were suddenly too busy looking for audience share. The murkier the story, the better. When I got into this, I never thought that the stories I would see my paper cover would be all about who was sleeping with whom. In fact, in the early days I buried a lot of those stories." He shook his head, making up his mind. He stepped back inside and returned after a few minutes holding a manila envelope.

"Guilt is the wrong reason to do anything. It forces us into making the wrong choices. We all make mistakes. All of us make decisions based on where we are in life at a particular time. Do what you need to do, but do it because it's right for you. Consider this my way of helping you."

She took the package from him and opened it. Her heart skipped a beat when she saw that it held pictures, but as she pulled them out, she saw that they were not what she had expected to see. Not by a long shot. She felt the shudder that went through her body and forced herself to look up from the photographs.

"When?"

"Three, four years ago, I think." He watched her steadily.

"How did you get these?"

He smiled and rubbed an index finger over his chin. "I know a lot of people. Being editor of a national paper sometimes has advantages. Everywhere I go, I get offers. I'm not above accepting minor bribes for doing some careless politician a favor. Sometimes, when I feel like it, I even get involved in kick-starting a foundering campaign just by what goes into my paper. Usually when I'm bored. This town is all about the 'you scratch my back, I'll scratch yours' trade-off. But I like to believe that I still have a shred of decency buried under all that. I get a lot of stuff that never sees the light of day." He nodded toward the envelope. "I thought this was irrelevant at the time."

He stood up from the patio chair, took a deep breath, and looked at her for a long while. "I've always liked you, Lauren. You've always handled yourself with class. It's rare in this town. Your affair will not break in my paper. If it breaks elsewhere, we will cover it, but we won't be the ones to break it. You have my word."

Her eyes filled with tears, understanding the ramifications of his stopping an investigation. "Thank you."

"But this is the last time you are allowed to use that night to obtain something from me."

"Understood." She leaned up and kissed his cheek. "You're a good man, Stephen."

"This entire conversation is off the record, including that last statement." He smiled at her. "Good luck, Lauren. I hope you get to where you need to be."

"You, too. You should follow some of your own advice."

"Lauren?" His voice stopped her in the doorway, and she turned. "You would have made a hell of a first lady."

Back in the car she sat stunned, unable to remember how she had walked out. She opened the envelope again and looked at the photos. She tried to feel something, anything, but it was as if she was frozen in the moment. The photos had been taken with a telescopic lens and so were a bit blurry, but there was no mistaking that they were of Matt kissing another woman. She couldn't bring up any sense of anger or betrayal or hurt; there was just a feeling of inevitability. They had been living separate lives for so long, there truly was no turning back for either of them. In a way she was angry with Stephen for giving her an out, a way of absolving herself of the responsibility for her actions. But the breakup of her marriage was not due to infidelity, hers or Matt's. The irony of the moment was not lost on her. *What a tangled web we weave*, she thought. *How sad for us.*

Chapter
Fourteen

"I want a separation."

Matt's face remained impassive, only the tightening of his jaw indicating he had heard her.

"A what?"

She didn't answer. He had heard her. She braced for the explosion, but he surprised her.

"Just like that? You woke up this morning and decided you wanted out?"

"It's been a long time coming, Matt. You've just been too busy to notice."

"Notice what? That my wife doesn't want what...exactly?"

"Matt, we haven't been happy in years."

"I've been busy building our future."

"That's just it. You've been busy building your future, not mine. Did you just once ask me if I wanted to be first lady?"

"I did."

"You didn't. You told me. Believe me, there is nothing wrong with your ambition; it's just not what I want for my life."

Matt was frustrated and, deep down inside, scared. "I don't get it. Is it because I don't tell you I love you often enough? I don't buy you flowers? What? Is it because I didn't take your therapy seriously? I'll go with you, if that will stop this nonsense."

She stared at him, overwhelmed by the loss she felt as she looked at him. "It's too late. I pleaded with you to come to therapy with me five years ago, and you didn't want to. You made fun of my request. Now you would only be going because I'm leaving you. You have to want to do it for the right reasons. And you know what? Those reasons are gone for me."

He was unable to comprehend that she really meant to follow

through, regardless of his feelings. "This is stupid. You know I love you."

"I know, Matt. But you love the idea of being president more. And it's no longer enough for me. It never was. I just didn't understand it then."

He opened his mouth to say more, but for the first time in their 13 years together, he saw something in her eyes that he instinctively knew meant he couldn't bend her to his will. "It's because of her, isn't it?"

She had dreaded the question. She didn't want this conversation about their relationship to be about Madison. But she also knew that she didn't want to lie anymore. "Matt, this isn't about anyone else. Yes, there was someone, but it's not about that. This is about you and me, and our wanting different things out of life. This is about needing more than what we have in order to be happy. Our relationship has been on autopilot for years; it's time to walk away." She could tell by the look on his face that he wasn't getting it, and felt panic rise. She knew that if she backed down, she would be lost. Whatever little part of herself she was trying to save would disappear into running a campaign and being the perfect politician's wife.

"What is it that you want? What is it about being married to me that makes you so unhappy?"

"It's not being married to you, Matt; it's how I feel." She took a deep breath, desperately trying to come up with words that would make sense, would get through to him. "I love you so very much, Matt. You have been in my life forever," she told him quietly, then took the plunge. "But I'm not in love with you. And now I know the difference. I'm in love with someone else."

He stood up then, angrier than she had ever seen him. His anger was more frightening because it was so controlled—no ranting or shouting, just sudden deadly calm. "Do you think you can just calmly say you want out now, months before the convention? It's bad enough that I have to find out that you betrayed me. If this gets out, I could be ruined. What do you think will happen if all of a sudden you walk out? Do you think the press is going to call off the hunt just because you're gone? Out of sight, out of mind? You know full well that you'll just be giving them ammunition to keep digging. *Newsbeat* especially will know something is up. Your leaving lends more credence to their story than any stupid document they have that could be a forgery. Until they can find enough to prove their allegations, they can't print them. But the minute they see anything different in our behavior, once they scent something, they won't stop at our separation." He dragged a hand through his hair, frustrated. "I shouldn't have to tell you this. You of all people should know what a powder keg we are sitting on. All because—" He stopped, realizing how much he was saying.

"All because of me," Lauren said quietly. "Say it, Matt. That's what you mean. If this blows up, I will be to blame for it all."

"You are not ruining this for me. I've got to get ready for a debate." Determinedly, he stalked out.

Later, Lauren was downstairs fixing herself a cup of tea when the doorbell rang. She wanted to ignore it, but when it rang again she marched to the door impatiently, swallowing the resentment when she recognized Clarence on the other side. "He's not here," she told him without preamble.

"I know. I wanted to talk to you."

Lauren turned and left him in the hallway to return to the kitchen. He followed her. "What about?"

"About this whole mess. How are you? How are you holding up?"

"Do you even care, Clarence?" Lauren turned to confront him. "Or are you fishing for something? I'm getting tired of beating around the bush. Just spill it, whatever it is. It must be important if you left him hours before the debate to come and check up on me."

Clarence smiled. Damn, she was great. "Truly, Lauren? I do care about you." Her snort was unladylike. "Lauren, do you think this is what I wished for you? For Matt? Regardless of what has passed between us, I have never wished you harm."

Lauren turned to him her eyes cool. "Oh, I know. You just want me to be the perfect little wife." She smiled then, without any humor. "What do you want, Clarence?"

His look sobered. "I want you to be there tonight."

"Have you talked to Matt about it?"

"No. I'm asking for his sake."

"You might want to check with him on that."

"Why?"

"Talk to Matt, Clarence."

"Does that mean you won't come?"

"No. I won't."

He was frustrated, trying to find a way to minimize the

impact of whatever would follow. Knowing that Matt was not at his best at the moment, he was trying hard to keep him on an even keel until after the debate. "Lauren, you have an obligation–" The minute the words were out of his mouth, he knew he had made a mistake.

She turned on him, eyes flashing. "Don't you dare lecture me about obligation. Not you. I've done nothing but meet my damn obligations."

"I know. I'm sorry," he offered.

"You of all people should know what this all has cost me. Do you think any of this has been my first choice?"

He sighed. "Lauren, we need you tonight especially. Matt, he's...he needs you."

Her eyes hardened. "I'm sick to death of being needed. *I* need me." She turned from him, despair rising. "Dammit, just go."

He hesitated, trying to find the words to plead, but failing. He turned to leave.

Lauren fought off the waves of resentment and felt the tightening grip of responsibility. Her voice stopped him at the kitchen entrance. "Clarence?" Lauren met his eyes. The look in them was sad; her heart was breaking for Matt. She knew that she would not back down from her decision, but the overwhelming guilt about hurting him and his chances was too fresh to turn him away. She felt weakened by her inability to stand strong against the pressure of his needs. She sighed. "I will go tonight. But it is the last time I will stand by him in public. It has to be. I think it's time we all got used to the idea. As soon as it can be arranged, I'm moving to the Cape permanently."

He nodded, then turned to leave.

Keith waited by the speakers' platform amidst the pool of reporters until Heather acknowledged him with her eyes. After the others had left, she walked slowly to him, eyes squinting in the sun. "Hey, Keith."

"I need to see the senator."

Heather frowned at him. "We are not doing one-on-ones this week. You will have to shout the questions out, the same as everybody else."

Keith smiled without humor. "The question I have for him is of a personal nature. I don't think he would want me to shout it from the rope lines." His tone was patient. "He's going to want to hear this in private."

Heather folded her arms, gazing at her feet. Carefully she asked, "Are we talking about some sort of illegal activity?"

She knows, Keith thought. *Somehow she knows to filter for him, to protect him.* His tone became harder. "No, but it is sensitive in nature. So, when do I get to see him?"

Heather looked up again, her eyes less friendly. "As soon as you tell me what it is."

"No dice. I'm trying to give him a chance, but I'm willing to go with what I've got on Monday." It was a bluff, but she didn't know it. If Keith was right, Lauren somehow had alerted them to his visit. He could imagine Heather calculations as she studied him. Did *Newsbeat* have enough to print?

"I'll think about it," Heather said finally. "And you can think about telling me more."

"Seventy-two hours," Keith repeated.

Hours before the debate, Clarence stood in the hotel room with Matt. He was bone tired. The pouches under his eye were more pronounced, his ulcer flaring up again. He was long overdue for a physical. He knew what the doctor would say: cut out the cigars and the cognac and lose twenty pounds. It was at times like these that he more acutely felt the madness in which they were engaged. He felt the sheer grind of endless hotel rooms, debates, and preparation. Tonight, Matt felt it too. Clarence looked over at the candidate. He looked edgy, distracted. Dressed in jeans and an Aerosmith T-shirt, he was lying on the sofa, his left foot bouncing nervously on the floor.

Matt was unnerved by his conversation with Lauren. He didn't have the emotional capacity to analyze his feelings and understand that what he felt was panic at the thought that his carefully crafted life was days away from imploding. He sat up abruptly. "She wants a separation."

Clarence was impassive, somehow unsurprised by the pronouncement. He turned to peer through the drab curtains at the dusk settling over the city. He could almost see his dream of becoming attorney general slipping through his fingers.

Matt turned to his oldest friend. "Did you hear me?"

"Yeah. I heard."

"I told her no." Matt raked his hands through his hair, a habit that indicated he was upset or anxious. "Jesus, she's going to fuck it all up."

Clarence stared down at the pedestrians hurrying across the street, people rushing home to their families, to dinner plans already made weeks in advance. So, there it was. He wasn't surprised that it had come to this. He flashed back to the night he had visited Lauren in the hospital room, the look on her face after his visit. What he had asked her then was to give up everything for his and Matt's ambitions. Only someone with the fever could ask others for that type of sacrifice. And yet she had done it. And he had no doubt that if the press hadn't come knocking with their questions, she would still be going along, at whatever cost to her. He sighed, the weight of it unsettled in his stomach. "Maybe a separation would be for the best, Matt." He was amused at himself for that. *Who would have thought I still had a shred of decency left in me?*

"What?"

"I'm pretty sure we can bury the story for a time. I'm not as convinced it can be hidden permanently. Regardless, we can't go through a grueling campaign with an absentee wife."

Matt slumped back down on the sofa, the enormity of what was being discussed settling on his shoulders. "She's my wife, Clarence. We've been together since university. I just..." His hands scrubbed at his face.

"Yeah, well, I was married for 26 years, until she decided she had had enough of waiting for me to show up for dinner. This life we chose is hard on anyone left behind." His tone was not unsympathetic.

Matt leaned back against the sofa and closed his eyes. "The fucked-up thing is that I love her."

Clarence crossed to him and placed his hand on his shoulder in a brief gesture of support. "I know. She loves you, too, or she wouldn't have stuck it out this long. Have you ever considered the idea that maybe she *is* gay?"

"No way." He was adamant about that, almost insulted, as if her being gay was a reflection on his own capability as a husband and a man. "Even if she was, people have discreet arrangements all the time."

Clarence rubbed his chin thoughtfully, feeling the stubble under his fingers. "Let's get you ready for the Meet the Press. We can talk about it later."

Matt stood and crossed to the bathroom. In the doorway, he turned to look at his friend, the look on his face brooding. "Did she ever tell you she was?"

"No, not in so many words. But then again, did we ever give her a chance to?"

Keith sat in his car munching on a bag of potato chips and half listening to the squawk noises coming from his police scanner. He was taking a moment before the debate was set to ponder his next moves. When his cell phone went off, he almost ignored it, but habit was a hard thing to break. "McGraw."

"Who the hell have you been talking to?"

The furious tone of his editor gave him pause. "What?"

"I don't know what the hell is going on, but I was called to the big man's office. He started asking all kinds of questions about your story. He wants to see your notes."

"He what?" Keith's mind raced as he tried to retrace his last movements and who he had talked to.

"Someone got to him. Whoever you've talked to has rattled some cages. Get your ass back into town, and bring all your notes."

Keith hung up. *Well, there it is.* He thought back over the past few weeks, trying to see where had he miscalculated. All he could think of was that either Lauren or Matt had somehow gotten to the editor. But even if they had contacted Stephen, why would he care? Stephen was no pushover, often thumbing his nose at the establishment just to show he could. In countless ways, the editor in chief had gone to bat for his reporters when he believed in their story. *So what happened on this one?* Keith suddenly worried that somehow his story would get buried. After many nights of fantasizing about his appearance on *Larry King Live* to discuss his scoop, he could see it all vanishing with this one phone call. For Keith, this moment was another one of those unavoidable truths. He was determined not to lose this one chance at the spotlight. He wasn't going to stand still and watch others decide his future. His imaginary taste of fame was too enticing to relinquish, no matter what anyone said. If *Newsbeat* was too timid to print the story, he would find somebody else who wasn't.

Matt and Clarence arrived at the studio. It was like all TV studios: cheap, sterile, and brightly lit, smaller than it appeared on the screen. The moderator, a well-known anchor for the evening news, was talking to Tom McLennan and his wife, and, of course, their two blond-haired children. *The perfect family,* Clarence thought bitterly. He glanced at Matt, wondering what he was thinking. Matt's attention, however, was focused on the first row of the audience. Clarence turned and saw Lauren sitting there alone. For a moment, Clarence thought that Matt would ignore her, and his eyes caught McLennan's interested look. But almost as if he had sensed something, Matt turned and crossed to her. He leaned down to kiss her cheek, aware of the scrutiny they were getting. "You came."

"Yes. Good luck, Matt." She looked up at him, her heart full of love and grief. He looked at her without saying anything else. In his eyes were confusion and anger. He turned from her and crossed to the desk where they would be sitting and shook McLennan's hands. The candidates stood there smiling as they made idle chat, pretending that this was their idea of fun, that they were not so gripped by tension that each body part felt screwed on too tight.

Oh, well, Clarence thought, *time to do my part,* and he headed for McLennan's campaign manager, ready to play his role in the charade. "Hello, Tony," Clarence said, shaking hands. "How are things?"

Above his thin smile, Tony Cronnor gave Clarence a quick, speculative glance. "Just dandy. Your man ready?"

"Oh, yeah."

Cronnor stopped smiling. "The country could do worse than either of those two. Things happen, though, and you have to go with it." His voice softened. "Tell Matt we're sorry about what we're going to have to do to him tonight. I don't know if he'll ever accept this, but it really isn't personal."

Against his will Clarence felt himself freeze, heard his own silence as he stared into Cronnor's ice-blue eyes. Was this a hint of what was to come? Cronnor glanced once at Lauren sitting on the other side and left. Clarence worriedly looked over at her and wondered how he could get her out of there. If his guess was accurate, she didn't deserve what was about to happen. *And I have to warn Matt.* Casting about frantically, he saw his candidate settling into his chair, an assistant clipping a tiny microphone to his lapel. *Too late.* His eyes found Lauren's and he forced a smile. The stage cleared, and the debate began.

Sitting to the left of the stage on Matt's side, Clarence checked his watch. *Twenty minutes to go, and we'll be out of this free-for-all unscathed.* As the debate wore on, Matt had become quicker, and every comparison he made was tied to a central theme—that he was the breath of fresh air, the innovator, and McLennan, tied to the previous administration, was too compromised to lead. But Clarence couldn't stop thinking of Cronnor's warning. The more Matt damaged him, the more desperate McLennan might become.

"Gentlemen," the moderator interjected, "as is my privilege, let me redirect this somewhat intense discussion of family issues to another subject that excites no emotion whatsoever: the rights of gays and lesbians."

The dry remark drew a smile from McLennan and, somewhat belatedly, from Matt. Watching the show, Lauren suddenly tensed as she recognized the strain on Matt's face. "As you both know, Congress recently narrowly passed the Defense of Marriage Act, barring same-sex marriages. Now Wyoming has introduced Proposition 24 which, if passed, would ban so-called 'special rights' for gays and lesbians." He turned to McLennan. "Starting with you, where do each of you stand on the issue of gay rights?"

McLennan leaned forward. "I oppose discrimination against citizens who pay taxes, hold jobs, and contribute to society. That means *any* citizen, regardless of sexual orientation." He turned to Matt. "You voted for barring same-sex marriages, and I was curious as to where that puts you on the issue of gay rights."

"Americans aren't ready to change the definition of marriage, which is thousands of years old and derives not from the government, but from the Old Testament. I did what I was elected to do. I listened to my constituents and voted against the bill." Matt shifted, wanting to get off the topic.

Clarence held his breath, praying that that would be the end of it.

McLennan leaned forward. "Listening to your constituents is admirable, but let's talk about something closer to home, then. What if someone close to you, someone you cared about, came to you and said they were gay; would you then speak in favor of gay rights?"

Matt stared at McLennan. Three feet separated them. For the first time, Matt could see the fear of losing etched on his opponent's face. McLennan seemed to hesitate, as if looking into an abyss. With a tense, terrible certainty, Matt thought, *It was you.*

For a last moment, McLennan looked as appalled as Matt felt, and then he pressed on in a tighter voice. "What if it was your wife?"

Lauren's face drained of color and she watched in horror as Matt's face froze at the question. The atmosphere suddenly had an electric feel to it as the audience held their breath. They were oblivious to the specifics of the dangerous undercurrents, only aware that something had shifted in front of them.

His eyes unconsciously found Lauren, and as their eyes met, she shook her head helplessly. "Is this the level to which we've sunk?" Matt asked softly, so softly that only McLennan and the moderator heard. "Should I ask if you still beat your wife?" Startled, McLennan blinked. Matt turned and his eyes held Lauren's. His voice was stronger. "I would hope that I would feel compassion. And love." Her eyes filled with tears. He turned to McLennan. "What if we ask the question differently? What if we ask people whether, because someone is born gay or lesbian, we're going to treat that person worse than everyone else? That's never been the kind of thing that Americans agree with." Matt felt calmer now. "I might not have agreed with the idea of *special* rights for gays and lesbians, only because I believed that they should have the same rights as anyone else."

For Lauren, the rest of the debate was a blur. Stunned by the moment, she didn't hear the closing arguments. She had almost been outed on national television! Then an alarming thought flashed through her mind. *Did Clarence know that might happen? Is that why he begged me to attend?* Her eyes searched around for him. Was that his way of ensuring she stayed, his own desperate way of putting pressure on her? He was ruthless enough, yet she couldn't quite believe that he would resort to those kinds of tactics, if for no other reason than that they were almost as damaging to Matt.

Amidst the applause that signaled the end of the debate, Matt waited for the sound system to switch off. He stood first, and extended his hand to McLennan. With a wan smile, McLennan took it, and then Matt moved closer. "Pray, Tom," Matt said under his breath. "Pray you can put the genie back in the fucking bottle. Because if you can't, I'm going to take everything I know about what happened twenty years ago and jam it up your ass." He went to Lauren, who stood shakily, and took her arm to escort her out without saying a word.

Clarence met them outside by the car. His face was tight, his eyes worried. "It was McLennan. It had to be."

Matt's face was impassive, but his voice was not. "I'm going to bury the fucker alive. I'll meet you at the house," he told Clarence. "I'm going back with Lauren." Startled, they both looked at him. Clarence and Lauren exchanged a look, then Lauren got in the car and Matt slid behind the wheel.

They drove a part of the way home in silence. Matt glanced at her. "Are you gay?" he finally asked.

Caught off guard by the question, she turned to him, an automatic denial on her lips. "I haven't had a chance to put a label on it," she answered cautiously.

"Are you really in love with her?"

Lauren turned in her seat to look at him. "Matt, do you really want to be having this conversation in the car?"

He glanced at her, then away. They drove the rest of the way home in silence. At the house he waited for her at the front door. "Thank you for being there tonight," he said, then he unlocked the door and stepped in.

She followed him. "Matt," she tried helplessly, "I do love you. You are my best friend. The thought of not having you in my life terrifies me. I wish things could be different."

He looked at her. "Me, too. I'm sorry it's been hard. I guess I never paid attention."

Lauren looked at him, at the man with whom she had shared her life for nearly fourteen years, and suddenly felt lost. He was such a good man deep down inside. "I'm sorry, too. I should have said something years ago when it might have been easier. I just didn't want to hurt you, hurt your chances. I was scared, and I didn't know what to do. I didn't know then what it would all end up meaning. And look at us now."

"If it was a man you were in love with, I would hunt him down and kick his sorry ass."

She looked at him and smiled slightly. "I know."

"I don't understand any of this," he said, frustrated. "Help me understand how you can be with me all of these years, and then wake up one day and be gay." His fingers snaked through his hair. "You don't look like a lesbian."

Lauren had to smile at that. "Do you know many?"

He turned to her and then had to smile at his comment. "Yeah, that was lame. Shit. I'm so fucked up over this, Lauren. I just wish I could understand why, what the hell happened."

"I wish I could too, Matt. This is not easy for me. Do you really think that this is where I wanted to end up when we got married? It just happened. One day, everything suddenly made sense." She turned, her hands pushing the hair from her face as she tried to explain something she barely understood herself. "It was like I was finally awake. But, Matt, you have to understand that our separation has nothing to do with my being with a woman. I am sorry that it seems that way. It would have happened regardless. I was not happy. The affair was more of a wake-up call that forced me to do some serious thinking about us and about who I am. And now, with the story probably coming out in the press, there is no reason to stay."

He threw his jacket over the back of a chair and frowned. "This is the worst kind of timing, Lauren. I don't know how to handle it. I've waited for my chance for years, and now, when I can almost taste it, you throw in a bomb like this."

She sighed, feeling the guilt rise, seeing in his eyes the resentment, the anger that she knew could change to hatred. "I don't know what else to do but leave, Matt. Let me make a clean break. We don't need to announce it yet. I'll move my stuff to the Cape. The longer this goes on, the longer we take a chance that it will come out later when we can't be proactive. There have been divorced presidents before. Reagan was divorced from Jane Wyman."

He looked over at her. "Yes, but he was married to Nancy when he was elected. And he didn't lose his wife because she preferred women."

Lauren paled, the words hitting home. "I'm sorry." She couldn't find anything else to add.

He was about to say something more, but was interrupted by the ringing of the doorbell. He hesitated, but as the doorbell rang a second time, he turned and left. At the door, he let Clarence in and they returned to the living room. He unknotted his tie, tired and wired at the same time. Images from the debate flashed through his mind: McLennan, the shock and fear on Lauren's face when the question had been asked, his own stunned disbelief at the sheer gall of it all. "McLennan?" he asked.

"Yep." Clarence sat across from him. "I spelled it out for them. They're very sorry."

"Of course." Matt turned and started to pace.

"They're laying off the topic and will return the notes to us."

"A little late for that now, don't you think, when the story is so close to breaking? They can't keep the reporters from digging further. Who the hell knows who else has a damn copy?"

Matt sank down on the couch facing Clarence. "We need to figure out what to do next, Clarence. This story won't stay buried." Clarence was about to speak, but stopped as Lauren entered the room.

"Don't bother, Clarence. This involves me just as much, if not more, than Matt. Whatever you two decide, I need to know."

Clarence glanced at Matt for confirmation, and he nodded. Lauren swallowed her resentment at that. Clarence started to pace. "I think we should lay low for a while, sound out the topic of a separation a bit. Maybe do a couple of polls. California is a key—"

Something in Lauren snapped. "Are you kidding me? Polls?" She crossed to stand in front of them, her eyes angry. Images of Madison, of her empty life crowded in, and she took a deep breath, steadying herself. It would not do to lose control now. "This is our life we are talking about. *Our* life. You don't decide what to do in your life by what the damn polls say. That is what is wrong with this whole campaign." She shook her head. "You both are so busy worrying about what the polls say that you have forgotten the message you were trying to get across. Well, I'm sorry, but that is not the way I want to live my life. I am moving back to the Cape. You can decide how to break the news, but I have to leave. I'm done living a lie."

"This is a big risk," Clarence tried to reason, as he looked at Matt.

Matt had been sitting hunched slightly forward, his forearms braced on his legs, holding his glass between his legs watching his wife. Now he jerked his gaze from her face and began idly rolling the glass between his palms, his jaw tightening.

"Yeah? Well it's my risk to take," Lauren snapped.

"Wrong." Matt stood up. "This isn't just about you. Do you

think that I want to stand in front of the press to answer questions about when I first knew that my wife was a dyke? Grow up, Lauren. This is not a game. And you can't just decide that you want out and think that we are all going to fall into line with your little plans." Matt turned to Clarence. "Give us a minute here, Clarence."

Clarence nodded. Satisfied that Matt would take care of the situation, he stepped out. Matt turned on Lauren, his face flushed with anger, the look in his eyes deadly. Unnerved by the anger and hatred she saw on his face, Lauren took a step back.

"I've told you before, Lauren, you will not ruin this for me."

She stared at him as if seeing him for the first time. In his rage, he looked like a stranger. Gone was the reasonable man of only an hour before. It was as if a switch had been thrown. "Matt—" she tried to reason.

"Enough, Lauren. You will be by my side if I have to drag you there personally."

She felt a mixture of anger, despair, and fear well up. She knew that there would be no reasoning with him tonight. She shook her head, her heart breaking for the both of them. All this time, and neither knew the other. His infidelity, hers—it was all so ugly and sordid. Worse, it was pointless. Should she tell him she knew of his affairs? She decided against it. Her leaving him had nothing to do with that; it would only confuse the issue further. She would not back down. She couldn't. She stared at him for a moment, then turned away. "I'm sorry you feel that way, Matt, but no, I will not be a presence in the campaign." With that, she left.

Darcy was drawing down a pint from the tap when her eyes caught the newest arrival at the door. She frowned at Lauren, who stood indecisively in the doorway.

Now that Lauren was here, she had no idea what she was going to do. She hadn't thought too far beyond getting away from Matt and Washington. She had thrown a few things in an overnight bag with the intention of hiding out in the Cape, but halfway into the flight, the need to talk someone had become overwhelming, and ironically the only one person she could think of was Darcy. So here she was. But now she wondered if it was a mistake.

"Jesus, you're like a bad penny who keeps showing up. In or out; stop blocking my door."

Lauren stepped in and crossed over to the bar. "Still charming, I see."

Darcy smirked as she fixed another drink and placed it on the bar for the server to pick up. "There's a coffee shop across the street," she told Lauren in an echo of an earlier visit.

Lauren sighed as her hand rubbed her eyes. "Give me something strong, will ya? When I'm done, I want to feel nothing."

Darcy raised her brows at that. "A blow to the head usually does the trick, and it can be less painful than a hangover."

"I'm sure you would like to volunteer to deliver the coup de grace." Lauren made a face and sat down on one of the black leather stools.

Darcy reached behind her and grabbed a bottle. "Ever had tequila?"

"Nope."

"Good." She poured her a shot and poured another shot next to it. When Lauren lifted her eyebrows at that, Darcy shrugged. "There is nothing more pathetic than a drunk sitting alone." Darcy stared at Lauren as she took a cautious sip. "For crying out loud, you don't sip tequila. Who does that? You are such a girl!" She took the shot glass and threw back her head and drank the tequila in one quick toss. She then smirked as Lauren, after a brief hesitation, did the same. She waited for the look of horror to spread as Lauren felt the drink burn a fiery path down her throat, but Lauren's face remained blank, then she slammed the shot glass down on the bar and raised a brow at Darcy. Darcy's mouth quirked. *Damn if I'm not starting to like this girl.* She poured another two.

Lauren lifted her glass in a toast. "Here's to pretty girls."

Darcy grinned. "And ugly ones." After about the third round, a warm mellow haze started to course through Lauren. Darcy continued to keep an eye on her as she poured drinks for other customers, washed glasses, and rang up sales. "Want to tell me what has you determined to puke in the morning?"

Lauren smiled. "You have such a way with words. It's a wonder that Ms. Right hasn't been swept off her feet yet."

Darcy smirked again as she poured two more. "What makes you think she hasn't? On their backs, that's where I like them best."

Lauren shook her head, trying to focus on Darcy, her tongue suddenly thick. "Sweet. What is it that we are drinking?"

"Heaven and hell all wrapped up in gold. Tequila Gold."

"Here's to having your heart broken," Lauren toasted. Darcy rolled her eyes. Not quite steady, Lauren placed her elbows on the bar. "Have you ever been in love?"

"Me? Yeah, tons of time."

Lauren continued to look at Darcy, her eyes almost pure gold. "No, I mean *really* in love." Because her head suddenly felt heavy, she rested it in her hand. "I didn't think it existed, you know? I thought that half the stuff you see in the movies is pure crap."

Darcy was amused. "Most of it is."

"Yeah. Except for this tiny part that no one warns you about. The French call it *coup de foudre.* It sorts of translates into 'lightning bolt,' which isn't a very good translation. It kind of means love at first sight."

"Is that what happened with Madison?" As soon as the words were out, Darcy wished she could pull them back.

Lauren didn't seem to mind the question. She toyed with her glass. "It wasn't quite at first sight. It was more like a nuclear meltdown over a couple of days." Her face grew pensive. "After spending one full day with her, I knew that I was in love with her and that I would never love another like that. It was like she was flowing through my veins."

There was a pause as they exchanged a look. Darcy shook her head. "Man, that's scary stuff. Too scary for me."

Lauren smiled. "For me, too." Darcy poured them another shot, and Lauren made a face but took it.

"That makes sense."

"What does?" Lauren tried to remember what they were talking about.

"You were scared about feeling too much, so you ran away from Madison, straight back to what was safe for you. Your husband."

"You a shrink, too? I thought it was only in movies that people spilled their guts to the bartender."

Darcy's smile was dry. "I have a degree in psychology and I own a café, so technically I'm not a bartender." Lauren tried to stand. Darcy, who had turned to rinse glasses, saw the movement from the corner of her eyes and frowned. "Where are you going?"

Lauren swayed. "To get a tattoo."

Darcy, who had been concentrating on pouring, stopped and turned. "Did you say tattoo?"

"Yeah. I've always wanted one. Right here on my hip bone below the bikini line."

Darcy hesitated. *Should I stop her? Damn it all, I'm not a babysitter.*

"Do they hurt?"

Darcy glanced at her, then grinned. "Darn right. I got one and—"

"You do? Where?" Lauren interrupted, curious.

"Never mind that."

Lauren had to sit again as everything seemed unsteady, including her balance. "I think I'm drunk. I don't remember the last time I got drunk. How did you do that? Give me another."

Amused, Darcy smiled at the woman swaying in front of her. It was easy to see the impact Lauren could have on anyone's peace of mind. She shook her head. "Try this instead."

It was coffee. Lauren sipped it, not noticing the difference, and continued the conversation as if her train of thought hadn't been interrupted. "You know the sad part? I only just figured out what happened: I've been going through the motions for too long, and I haven't a clue how to change things. I didn't trust enough in what she was feeling for me. I thought it was too good to be true, and I ran for cover. To give myself over so completely scared the hell out of me." She placed her head down on the bar and closed her eyes.

"Being first lady doesn't?" Darcy asked over her shoulder, amazed. "Lauren? Lauren?" Not getting a reply, she turned to Lauren, who had started to snore softly. She had passed out on the bar. "Women." *Now what? I can't just leave her here.* She went around the bar. "Come on, you can crash at my place tonight." She half carried Lauren out to the back where a separate entrance led up to an apartment she kept. After much fumbling, they staggered up the stairs and inside. She pushed her to the bed, and Lauren fell face down and lay unmoving. Darcy stared at her, baffled as to what her next step should be. The woman who could very well be the next first lady of the United States was passed out on her bed. She pulled her shoes off and settled a blanket over her.

Lauren stirred only long enough to open her eyes. "I'm going to be sick."

The look of horror on Darcy's face would have been comical if there had been anyone there to witness it. "Oh, for crying out loud." She lifted Lauren up and dragged her to the bathroom where she stood holding back her hair as Lauren threw up in the toilet. Darcy stared up at the ceiling, her stomach roiling. "Ewww..." *Serves me right, feeding tequila to a rookie like that. And my best stuff, too.* She wet a cloth and wiped Lauren's face and helped her back to bed.

Lauren collapsed onto the bed. "Sorry, Darcy."

"Forget it. I should have known you were too wimpy to drink. Why on earth would you want to get drunk? You're too goody-goody."

Lauren couldn't even find the strength to snap back. "I left Matt." Her eyelids felt too heavy to keep open, so she closed her eyes.

Darcy stared at her. "Wow! Well, that explains it." She went and rummaged through her kitchen for a pail, which she placed beside the bed. "If you feel like being sick again, do it in the bucket. Don't you dare throw up in my bed. These are my good Ralph Lauren sheets."

"You're very sweet."

"Don't get used to it." Darcy waited until it looked like Lauren was asleep before softly starting out.

At the door, Lauren's voice stopped her. It sounded young and defenseless in the dark. "Thanks, Darcy. I don't really have any friends I can talk to about her."

"Forget it. Go to sleep."

Back down in the bar, Darcy put the glasses away and thought of the woman upstairs. Man, she was getting soft. The ringing of the phone interrupted her thoughts. She crossed to the end of the bar and picked up the receiver. "Murphy's."

"Still pining away for me?" The familiar voice was cheerful.

Darcy stood frozen, shocked at the timing. She caught herself looking around guiltily. "Yeah, I pine for you every day."

"I have no idea why, but I was thinking about you tonight, so thought I would give you a call. How are things?"

"You have no idea." Darcy leaned against the wall, amazed that she should feel guilty for doing the right thing.

Madison heard something in her voice. "Are you okay?"

"Oh, yeah. Peachy."

"I was thinking of popping by for a drink—"

"Listen, Maddie, that might not be a good idea," Darcy interrupted.

"Why not?"

"I'm going to tell you something, but I don't want you to jump to the wrong conclusions."

Madison puzzled over the direction of the conversation. "Okay..."

"I think you should know that Lauren Taylor is sleeping upstairs in my apartment."

There was a long pause. "I'm sorry; for a moment there I thought you said Lauren was asleep in your bed."

"I did." She braced herself. It didn't take long.

"Are you fucking kidding me? What the hell is going on?"

Darcy made a face at the raised voice on the other end. "It's a long story. I think she is going to need a friend over the next few weeks."

"Since when are you two friends?" The voice was furious. Underneath the heat were emotions too complex to analyze.

"Since never. She showed up at the bar earlier and we had a few tequilas, and she passed out on the bar. I moved her to my bed."

"She passed out on the bar? Why would she be drinking tequila at your place? Darcy?" Madison was beside herself trying to cope with all of the feelings the news was stirring in her.

"Like I said, it's a long story. I'll tell you about it sometime. I'm going to keep an eye on her. I just thought you would like to know." For a moment, Darcy wanted to tell Madison that Lauren had left Matt, if only to relieve the pain. But it wasn't up to her. She had wanted Madison to know Lauren was not alone, just in case the separation was in the morning news, but hearing the turmoil in her friend's voice, she realized it had been a mistake to mention anything at all. She panicked, wanting to get off the phone before she caused more damage.

"Darcy, what is going on?"

"Nothing, Maddie; I swear. I'll talk to you later." Darcy hung up the phone, then spent a few minutes swearing at her stupidity.

"She's in Darcy's bed. She got her drunk on tequila. Jesus."

Alex stepped aside as Madison brushed by, her eyes wild. With a sigh, she closed the door then turned, trying to follow the conversation. "Who is?"

Madison turned accusing. "Did you know something was going on with them?"

Alex folded her arms across her chest, her tone mild. "If I knew what you were talking about, I might be able to answer."

"Lauren!" Madison turned, her eyes filling. "Never in a million years would I have imagined Darcy and Lauren." She was almost hysterical.

Alex studied her, surprised by the accusation. She crossed to her and pushed her down onto a chair, then shoved her head between her legs. "Breathe."

Madison fought against the firm hold. "Let me go, you ass."

"Dammit, I said breathe." Alex held her down until Madison took a deep breath. Then she released her and sat beside her. "Now, why don't you start at the beginning?" When she was finished, Alex looked thoughtful. It wasn't like Darcy to cross any lines; there had to be more to it. *God, I hope for all our sakes there is.* "Madison, Darcy said it was a long story. We should give her the benefit of the doubt."

"Alex, I don't know what I would do if Darcy and Lauren..." She shook her head, unable to even go there. "It's bad enough to let her go because she's married, but to think that she would take up with another woman..."

"Don't jump to conclusions," Alex soothed. *I'm going to kill Darcy,* she thought. *I'm going to go and shoot her dead.* "If she said there is an explanation, there is an explanation. Let me find out what it is."

Darcy was stacking bottles on the glass shelf when her eyes were drawn to the door. She sighed as she recognized the dark-haired woman. "Ah...here comes the cavalry." She reached up and placed another bottle, then turned.

"How's it going, Darcy?"

"Fine; you, Alex?"

"Want to tell me what's going on?"

Darcy's back was up immediately. She frowned. "News travels, I see."

"Madison was hysterical after talking to you. I don't know what to think."

"You don't?" That hurt. *Doesn't anyone give me any fucking credit?* Her eyes heated. "Bully for you." She turned to stalk back to the kitchen.

Alex's hand's was firm on her arm as she stopped her. "Darcy,

I will apologize if I am wrong, but I am at a loss to explain to one of my best friends how the woman she loves ended up in the bed of someone she barely knows. Someone who should know how raw this whole situation is."

Darcy angrily shook the hold off. "Who the hell do you take me for?" Her hands clenched.

Alex saw it and smiled, unperturbed. "Want to take a swing at me, Stretch?" The nickname was an old one, left over from the days when they had once dated. It eased the tension somewhat.

Darcy blew out a breath. "Hell, the whole thing is slightly left of the Twilight Zone, Alex."

Alex raised a brow. "Spill it. Or I might have to shoot you dead."

"Want a drink?"

"As long as it's not tequila," Alex answered dryly.

Darcy reached down and grabbed two beers from the cooler. She came around and sat on the stool beside Alex and handed her one. They both twisted off the caps in silence. "She showed up at the bar, all upset. Not crying upset, just emotional upset. She wanted to get drunk. So..." She shrugged. "We had a few tequilas, and the next thing you know, she's talking about falling in love with Madison and how scared she had been, and then she was going to get a tattoo." Alex gave her a look. Darcy saw it and nodded in silent agreement. "I told you it was weird. I wasn't really paying attention to how drunk she was getting, you know. I was working and all that; one minute she's talking, and then the next she's passed out on the bar." She stretched her long legs. "I carried her upstairs, helped her when she puked, then put her to bed. She left her husband, that's why I told Madison. Not that she left him, just that she was here. I thought maybe the papers would be all over it in the morning, and Madison might try to find her or something." She took a long gulp of the brew. "Big mistake."

"Big mistake," Alex agreed. "But I'm glad I don't have to shoot you dead."

"Me, too."

"Where do you want this box?"

"What's it labeled as?" Lauren stood, massaging the knot in her lower back.

"Mmm..." Darcy peered at the box she was holding. She

grinned. "Stuff."

"Stuff?" Lauren groaned, pushing a hand through her thick blond hair. "Stuff?"

"S-t-u-f-f. Yep. Stuff. That's what it says. Right here on the side." Darcy kept a straight face.

Lauren looked at her. "You're enjoying this, aren't you?"

"Me? Nah. Never." She tried an innocent look.

Lauren shook her head, then she gestured toward the pile by the living room. "I guess you can put it with the rest of them." They were all labeled "stuff."

"If it helps any, it sounds like breakables."

Lauren made a face. "I was in a hurry to leave." After the night of drinking at Darcy's, she had stayed at the Cape for a couple of days, then returned home to find Matt had left to go campaigning. Within a week, she had her things packed and her move arranged. Perhaps it was being sick in front of someone that had left her no dignity, but somehow since that night at Darcy's, they had bonded, striking up a friendship for which she was very grateful. Darcy was now there, helping with the unpacking. "I need a drink. Where's that wine you brought us?"

Darcy crossed to the kitchen and returned with a large bottle and two plastic cups. Lauren took it from her, then turned. "I wonder where I put the corkscrew?"

"Probably in the one labeled 'stuff,'" Darcy answered, lips twitching.

"Funny." Lauren turned back to the kitchen and returned with a corkscrew.

Darcy looked around with interest. "God, this house is breathtaking. Why didn't you live here more?"

Lauren concentrated on pouring the wine into the glasses. "Matt wanted us to live in Washington most of the time." She handed Darcy a glass, then gently tapped hers against it. "Cheers." She looked around. "This is where Madison and I spent most of our time. After it ended, I couldn't stand being here with all the reminders of her. It was easier to close the house for a while." Looking wistful for a moment, she glanced at Darcy, then away. "Have you talked to her recently?"

Darcy frowned. "Lauren..."

"Yeah, I know; sorry. That wasn't fair. I don't want you to feel like I'm using you for information." She turned back to the boxes. "Well, might as well start opening some."

Darcy hesitated. "She knows I'm spending time with you."

That stopped Lauren, who turned back to her. "How is she?"

The look on her face was raw and Darcy had to look away, unable to face such naked longing. "About the same as you, I would imagine...just trying to live her life."

Later that week Lauren sat cross-legged on her bed, talking to her older sister Anne. It reminded her of all of the nights when they were younger and had shared a room. In between all of their fights, they had had a lot of talks.

"So what happened, Lauren? Why did you run away?"

"I didn't run away exactly, I just..." Lauren sighed. "I just walked out of my life."

"But why?" Her sister was curious. "Was I so wrong when I thought you were happy?"

"No. There were a lot of good days. But the bad ones just started to outnumber the good ones." She shrugged. "I fell out of love, Anne. And I woke up one day and realized that the last few years of my life I have just been going through the motions. I have spent all of these years trying to be something I wasn't. I am not meant to be a politician's wife." She took a deep breath. "I am not meant to be a wife." Her sister still looked puzzled, so Lauren tried to explain the conflicting emotions she had felt. "All the time I was trying to be the type of wife that Matt wanted, I was burying who I really am. I decided it was time that I looked after *my* needs for a change. I want to start painting again. I want to be able to walk out of my door and see water and smell the fresh air. And I want to take the time to find out what I want, what I'm all about." She smiled. "That's all."

"That's all?" Her sister looked at her for a long moment. "There are things about you I don't understand, things going on inside of your head I just don't get. But this....it's hard to comprehend walking out on 14 years of marriage because you want to paint." She lifted her hand to forestall Lauren's objection. "I know, I'm simplifying it. Still..." She frowned. "What's really going on?"

Lauren looked down at the coverlet and felt the heaviness in her chest. Panic and fear, she guessed. She hesitated. "Anne, all these years, I thought I was in love with Matt. That what we had was all there was. I felt empty inside, and I didn't know why." She smiled a little. "Then I woke up one day and realized that that wasn't it at all, there was more."

"Lauren, are you saying there is someone else?"

Suddenly afraid of taking the next, irretrievable step, Lauren looked away. She turned to her sister and read the concern in the identical golden eyes and a calm came over her. "In a manner of speaking."

"Who is he?"

"It's not a he."

Anne released a breath, trying to hide her shock. "A woman? Are you trying to tell me that you fell for a woman?"

"Yeah. Head over heels, in fact."

"When did this happen, how?"

"Almost four years ago. I haven't been with her in over two years."

Anne frowned. "Let me get this straight..." Lauren's nervousness broke and she giggled at her sister. Anne stared at her, puzzled, then made a face as she got it. "No pun intended." They laughed softly, relieving some of the tension. "You're telling me that four years ago you fell for a woman, you haven't slept with her in two years, and you are only now leaving your husband— who is running for the presidency, by the way—because of it?"

Put like that it sounded crazy. "Yeah, that about sums it up."

"I see." She stood up, needing to pace. "Does Matt know the reason you left?"

"Yes, he does. At least, he knows about the affair, and he knows that I have left. He also knows that I had been thinking about leaving him long before I fell in love with a woman. Part of the reason I told him at this particular time is that the story is about to break in the papers any day now. It might affect his campaign."

Anne stared at her and Lauren had to laugh at the look on her face. "You don't do anything halfway, do you?"

"I guess not. It takes me a while, but once started there's no stopping me."

Anne tried to assimilate everything that she had heard. "Is this the first— I mean, was there—" She stopped, looking at her sister as if seeing her for the first time.

Lauren smiled, relieved that her sibling seemed calm about the whole thing. "It is the first time I've been with a woman, yes. But not the first time I've thought about it. I have felt attractions over the years."

"Who is she? Anyone I know?"

"She is a doctor; and no, you wouldn't know her. Anyway, she doesn't want me anymore, so this move is less about her and more about me."

Anne frowned. "What do you mean she doesn't want you?" Her loyalty to her sister was winning out over the reservations she was feeling. "Who wouldn't want you?"

Lauren smiled. "It's a very long story. Maybe I'll tell you one day."

They stared at each other. "Okay." There was a pause. "Look, Lauren, I don't pretend to understand this. And I don't know if I'm okay with it. One day you're married, the next you're gay. It's a little too much information to take in all at once. But you are my sister, so..." She shrugged.

"So you're stuck with me."

"Something like that."

They smiled at each other.

Madison sat at one of Darcy's tables, brooding over the turn of events. Jealousy was an unfamiliar emotion for her, and she felt it now in spades. The idea that Darcy was spending time with Lauren was weighing heavily on her, and she didn't know what to do about it. While she thought about it, she toyed with her glass of wine, her long, slender fingers twirling her glass, unable to be still. She felt unbalanced, as if the whole world had tilted on its axis. She fought off the waves of anger and resentment that washed over her when she saw Darcy come in from the back. It was the first time she had seen her friend since hearing about Lauren spending time with her, and her eyes heated as she took in the long-legged redhead. *Does she have to look so damn good?*

Darcy caught the glare and sighed as she hesitated in the doorway. She recognized the resentment, and for a moment she felt her own anger flare at the unfair position she was in of having to defend herself for no reason. She took a deep breath, then crossed to the table. It was her place, after all. "Hey."

Madison's fingers stilled and she let go of her glass as she looked up at Darcy. "Hey."

"Haven't seen you in a while." Darcy stood hesitantly by the table, her look cautious.

Madison watched her and was surprised by the uncertainty. It was so unlike Darcy that she was thrown by it. She sighed as she waved toward the chair in front of her. "Sit down. You make me nervous standing over me like that, Stretch." The affectionate nickname was automatic, but it softened the edges a bit and Darcy sat down.

"Listen–" they both started at the same time, and each laughed nervously. "You go," Madison finally said.

"Madison, you know that I love you and I would never do anything to hurt you, right?"

They stared at each other and Madison's eyes filled. The darn thing was she *did* know that. "I know."

"Nothing is going on. I mean between Lauren and me. These past few weeks, she needed a friend. And somehow, due to a chain of very unusual circumstances, I was there. And even though we were not friends then, we are now. But if it's too much for you, if my being friends with Lauren will affect *our* friendship, then I will stop spending time with her. You mean way too much to me to have you be mad at me all the time." Darcy looked near tears as she finished. Fiercely loyal to her friends, she was upset to think that she would be the cause of her friend's pain.

Madison looked past Darcy's shoulder at the bar, knowing that she could ask that of her friend and Darcy would be true to her word. It did not make her proud that there was a part of her that wanted to ask. But another part of her knew that it was selfish of her to insist that her friends should stay away from Lauren. She wanted Lauren to have friends. She hadn't quite realized before now how sharing her friends with Lauren would affect her. Over the last two years, as if by tacit agreement, her friends had never brought up the subject of Lauren. It was naïve of her to believe that Alex or Jamie, for instance, never spoke to Lauren, as they were her friends too. She felt somewhat diminished by her jealousy. It felt too much like high school. "No, don't do that. I'll get over it. I didn't realize how weird it would be, that's all. But I don't want you to stop being friends with her. That's dumb."

Darcy met her eyes and smiled. "Okay."
The pause between them was quieter, the nerves gone. Then Madison looked thoughtfully at Darcy for a moment. "What did you mean by 'she needs a friend'? What's going on? Is she okay?" The concern for Lauren was automatic.

Darcy silently cursed her unconscious slip. This was getting to be an unfortunate habit. She looked into the troubled smoky eyes in front of her and shrugged helplessly, taking the plunge. "She left Matt a few weeks ago. That's why she was here drinking that night. And last week, I helped her move out of her place and into her home out on the Cape."

The news hit Madison squarely in her midsection and she stopped breathing for a moment. Her hands stilled on the table as the shock carried through her system. She looked at Darcy, stunned. "She left him? I haven't seen that in the news."

Darcy nodded. "She's keeping a low profile. She's pretty shook up about it and fighting with him daily. He's angry. He's making all kinds of noise about needing her back for the campaign."

"Why didn't she call me?"

"Madison, be fair. After your last conversation, did you expect her to? I think she's trying to get her life in order first, without putting any pressure on you."

"She told you about that?" Madison frowned, uneasy that she was being discussed. Something that was incredibly private was now, it seemed, out in the open.

"She didn't have to. It's so clear."

Madison sighed and one hand rubbed tiredly at her eyes. "I thought I was over her, you know? I mean, I was finally ready to meet other women and then boom, she's back in my life and I'm right back where I was two years ago. I haven't made any progress in moving on. I want her so much, I hurt from it. I don't know what to do."

Darcy studied her for a moment, then decided to be blunt. "Don't do anything. She needs time to grieve for her marriage and for the life she's leaving. When and if she is ready, she'll come to you. If it's meant to be, it will be."

Madison shook her head. "When did you start being wise? The Darcy I know would have told me to get off my ass and go after her."

"Yeah. I guess I'm maturing or something. Fuck, I hope that doesn't mean I'm getting old." They started to laugh. Darcy stood up. "Are we okay?"

Madison followed her up and went to her, putting her arms around her. "We are okay." She kissed her. "Thanks for being there for her, Stretch. She could do a lot worse."

"You bet. Hang in there, Madison. Life has a way of working

out the way it should."

Madison smiled sadly. "That's something Lauren used to say."

Chapter
Fifteen

About a week later, shortly before noon, Lauren was interrupted by a call. She hit the flash button.

"Lauren Taylor?"

It was a man's voice, high-pitched and, to Lauren's ears, invasive. "Yes?" she answered tightly.

"This is Donald Roy." Startled, Lauren took a moment to steel herself, feeling surprise turn to dread. Given the circumstances, a call from the gossip columnist was something to fear. In an even tone, mustered with difficulty, Lauren inquired, "What can I do for you, Mr. Roy?"

"I'll get right to the point. We know about your affair with Madison Williams, and I'm about to go with it on-line. I thought you'd want to comment before I do."

Sickened, Lauren felt her hope of protecting Madison—and to a certain extent, Matt—slip away. "Not to you," she said softly.

It was twilight before Madison arrived at her best friends' home. The message from Alex had been cryptic and unnerving. *Don't go home or answer the phone, just come over. Take the subway if you can.* As Madison crossed their driveway, the front door opened to reveal a strained-looking Alex. "What's going on?" Alex didn't answer, but pulled her in.

"Alex, you are starting to scare me a little."

"Madison, something happened today. Go into the living room and we can explain."

Puzzled, Madison threw her a questioning look, then as she was stepping into the living room, she froze as both Megan and

Lauren stood up. Madison's eyes took in their worried faces, the evidence of tears on Lauren's face, and felt her heart drop. "What's going on?"

Without thinking about what she was doing, Lauren crossed to her former lover and into her arms. Madison's arms automatically went around her to hold her tight, and she felt Lauren's warm breath against her neck. Her eyes glanced worriedly over at Megan, who shook her head at the unspoken question. Megan stepped out of the room to give them some privacy.

"I'm so sorry. I promised myself I wouldn't cry." Lauren pulled back to look at her shakily. "Madison, it's out."

"What is?"

"Us. I got a call this morning to tell me that the story is breaking tomorrow on-line. It's only a matter of time after that before the press feeding frenzy follows. I don't know why I'm so surprised it is out. " She paced, her hands pushing the hair from her face. "I didn't know what else to do. I haven't told anyone else yet, including Matt. I badgered Darcy until she told me where you were, and then I just called Alex looking for you, and though I tried to explain why I needed to see you, by the time I was finished I'm sure I didn't make sense. I was babbling and—" She gave a short, choked laugh. "Just like now. She told me to come over, and here I am."

Madison looked at her—noting the strain on her face, the hint of panic in her eyes—and smiled gently at her, a calm settling over her. "This is where you should be, where you belong." She touched her face and Lauren's eyes closed at the soft caress, leaning into it.

"All I could think about was that I needed to find you."

Madison closed her eyes at that, helpless to repress the feelings that were flooding in.

Later they sat side by side on the couch, leaning into each other out of unconscious habit with Alex and Megan facing them as they tried to figure out what to do. "Do you think it's that reporter friend of yours? The one who came to you with the story?" Alex asked, the years of being a detective kicking in.

"Maybe. I don't think so. I do believe that somehow the leak comes from the same source. Maybe that is where we need to start. I need to get to Keith and talk to him, see what he knows and how far he got with his investigation. Maybe he talked to too many people." She looked exhausted, the stress finally catching up with her. "I need to call Matt, too." She stood up, looking down at Madison. "I'm not sure what will happen next. It could get really ugly for all of us. I'm so sorry."

Madison eyes took in the smooth profile, those incredible golden eyes that had haunted her for months, and knew that tomorrow she would plead insanity. "Stay here with me tonight. Tomorrow will come soon enough. We can figure something out then." If that startled Alex or Megan, they didn't show it as they made noises about getting the other guest room ready, then quickly disappeared.

Lauren turned and looked at Madison for a long moment. "I have missed you—more than you could possibly imagine, but staying here tonight may not be a good idea."

Madison nodded. "It probably isn't."

"I mean, weren't you the one who told me the other day that we couldn't start anything again? 'The vultures would pick our bones,' I think, were your exact words."

Madison smiled at that. "I did. But the vultures are about to come out with the story regardless of our next move. I'm offering you a hideout for the night until we can come up with a plan. That's what friends do."

"I see. Friends, huh?"

Madison looked at her, trying to gauge her mood. "Always. And you are still married, so..." She shrugged, unwilling to analyze the situation further.

Lauren looked at her, trying to read her face, but it was still shuttered. "We are separated, but technically yes, I am still married; but—"

"Lauren, do you want to stay?"

"More than I want to breathe."

"Then stay. Go call Matt."

Alex walked back in on that. "The room is ready, second door on the left."

With a quick glance at Madison, Lauren turned to Alex. "Thank you. I need to make a call. Is there somewhere I can go?"

"The kitchen in the back, wall by the fridge."

Lauren glanced at Madison, the look in her eyes soft, then left. Madison released a breath she didn't know she had been holding.

"Whatever you're thinking, this is not a good idea," Alex started.

"Probably not."

"Remember the last time..."

"I know, Alex. I'm well aware of everything." Madison's tone was dry.

"I just don't want you hurt again."

"It's got nothing to do with that, Alex. I'm involved no matter what I do. Because of then, because of now." Madison turned at a sound from the entrance, but it was only Megan returning. "Guys, stop looking at me like that," she finally said. They continued to look at her, their concern evident. "Did you see the way she looked at me?"

Megan smiled gently. "Yeah, we saw."

"Well, that look pretty much sums it up for me. What else can I do? How the hell am I suppose to walk away from her again?"

Later Madison stood in the bedroom, suddenly nervous. *What was I thinking? I should just leave her here and go back to my house.* Then her heart stuttered as the door opened and Lauren stepped in.

"Hi."

"Hi, yourself. Everything sorted out?"

"I couldn't reach anyone. They are campaigning in New Hampshire. I guess I will have to try tomorrow. By then, they'll know. I left a message with Matt to warn them."

"Did you tell Matt where you are?"

"No." Lauren continued to look at her. "I wanted it to be just us tonight. Tomorrow I will be owned by the world, all the sordid details on the Internet for everyone to pore over." Her tone was bitter. Lauren walked over to the window to look into the blackness, peering at the stars.

"God, I had forgotten how very beautiful you are," Madison told her quietly, the words out before she could think about them.

Startled, Lauren turned to her. She gave her a long look as if to see beyond the words. "Madison?"

"Mmm?"

"Is there anyone that will be worried if you don't get home tonight?"

Madison understood the question behind the words. "No,"

she sighed. "And before you get the courage to ask, there have been a few women over the last two years and none of them meant anything. I guess you spoiled me for anyone else." She smiled ruefully as they stared at each other, fighting their history. "We should talk about what to do next. I'm sure tomorrow will be madness. I don't really know what to expect."

"Depends on what kind of a news day it is. If everyone is bored, covering the same thing, they'll run with it. Being here in Boston instead of Washington might help for the first few hours, I would think. They will have to find you first. As for me, I will have to make an appearance somewhere. No one knows about the house on the Cape; I hope I can keep that hidden. Maybe it would be best if I avoid it for a while." She was thinking out loud. She turned to Madison, who stood by the door, and stared at her, mouth slightly open as if suddenly she was out of breath.

The impact of being in a room with Lauren again was overpowering, and she felt her whole body reacting. Something in her eyes had Madison's senses humming, her blood warming. She found herself unable to look away. Without saying anything else, they moved at the same time, then Lauren's mouth fused itself to hers. Someone groaned as Madison's mouth parted to allow Lauren's tongue to slip in to wildly pursue her own. Madison's hand buried itself in the blond hair, pulling her closer, letting the wildness in her soul triggered by being this close to the one she loved overcome any of the reservations she might otherwise have felt.

Lauren fell back against the door, her hands almost desperate in her haste to get at Madison's silken skin. They stumbled to the bed, mouths locked, and it was as if something was unleashed in Lauren. "Let me feel you. Oh God, honey, let me get to you." All those months of lying awake at night, her body on fire as it craved Madison's presence, burying her need. All those nights of picturing Madison beside her, seeing the curve of her neck, the gentle swell of her breasts, until the yearning was like a physical ache, seemed to snap the thin leash of her control. She was like a woman possessed. There wasn't any gentleness or tenderness— that would come later; for now there was only raw need.

Madison matched the explosion. Lauren's mouth and hands teased and heated Madison's body. In their haste, there was no time for delicacy. The sound of ripping, stark in the quiet, was ignored. Lauren's mouth closed on one nipple, then the other, tongue and teeth drawing the low, low moan that was so much a part of her memories of this woman. Lower, her mouth searched, remembering the scents, the textures that had haunted her. Then with a low growl, she plunged one, then two fingers into the heated wetness, her tongue following. And with mouth sucking wildly, teeth biting, nipping, fingers plunging deep, she threw Madison over the top almost immediately.

The cry was one of pent-up release as Madison's fingers grabbed hold of Lauren's head to press her closer to her shuddering center, holding her tightly as her entire body convulsed. "Oh, my God!"

But Lauren wasn't finished. Even with her own clitoris swollen and throbbing for release, she would not relent, and her mouth and fingers continued their assault until Madison came again with a wild thrashing that almost pulled them off the bed. Lauren gentled her mouth and continued to suck the sensitive skin, leaving Madison sobbing below her.

"Honey, come here. Let me hold you," Madison gasped.

Lauren moved to lie on top of her, groaning as her wet center connected with Madison's firm thigh. Her tongue, still full of Madison's taste, gently licked hot tears. Madison lay quietly below her, holding on tight until her shudders eased, and slowly she opened her eyes to look at Lauren, who was watching her with an intent look that was achingly familiar. Lauren's fingers touched Madison's mouth, and for a long moment they lay there staring at each other, unable to look away.

"I love you. I've always loved you," Madison whispered, undone by the moment.

At the soft words, Lauren came with a long, shuddering breath. Stunned that she could be brought to climax by the quiet words, she started to cry, her face buried in Madison's neck. She was finally home again. At last.

The next morning, Madison quietly padded down the stairs to make coffee and try to collect her thoughts. Hair tumbled down to her shoulders, robe worn loosely, she stood staring at the cupboard without moving, unable to get her mind to engage enough to comprehend the previous twenty-four hours. *Did last night really happen? Is Lauren really asleep upstairs?* She felt the pleasant lethargy in her legs that spoke of a night spent making love, yet she was almost afraid to confirm it. A hand moved past her to open the cupboard door and grab the coffee filters, startling Madison, who jumped back with a squeak. Madison stared at Alex as if seeing a stranger.

Alex raised a brow at the surprised look on her face. "What? I live here." She then concentrated on measuring the coffee. "You want coffee?" Not getting a response, she turned to Madison, who was still standing in the same spot staring into space. Alex waved a hand in front of Madison's bemused face. "Earth to Madison."

Madison shook her head. "Sorry, I was thinking."

Alex shrugged. "Whatever. Is Lauren still sleeping?"

"What?" Madison blushed furiously.

"Is— Wait a minute." Alex noticed the blush. "Look at me."

"Have I ever told you you're bossy?" Madison tried to avoid her eyes.

Alex's hand grabbed hold of her chin, forcing her eyes back to hers. "Did you and Lauren...? Of course you did. It's like throwing a lit match in a dynamite factory," she answered herself. Her face showed concern. "Was that wise?"

"You know what, Alex? Right now I can't seem to care whether or not it was wise. I'm in love with her. I can't do a damn thing about it. I tried, and it doesn't matter if I never see her again—I would still go on loving her."

Alex's hand was gentle against her face. "I know you would. And she loves you, too. It's pretty obvious to anyone with half a sense the way she looks at you, but I'm just worried for the both of you," she was quick to add. "Your affair with her is about to break in the tabloids, and starting anything this way will not only give them ammunition, it will be difficult for you guys to manage to have something normal, at least for a while. Relationships are hard enough to maintain without having the added pressure of doing it in front of millions. And there is still her husband to take into account."

"She left him, Alex. She left Matt months ago; they just haven't announced it."

Alex stared at her, still concerned. "I love you both. I don't want anything to happen to you. I don't want to see either of you hurt again."

"I know. I appreciate your concern, kiddo, but this is where I want to be."

"Want to be where?" a voice broke in.

Madison turned to Lauren, who had woken up alone and

gone searching for Madison, afraid that she had dreamt it all. Their eyes met. Lauren's long blond hair was a tousled mass and her face was still flushed from sleep as she stood staring at Madison. Madison thought she had never seen anything more beautiful in her life. "I woke up and you weren't there. It scared me," Lauren told Madison softly. It was as if it was just the two of them in the room, their focus so narrow that Alex could only watch in amused silence. She had never felt more like a third wheel.

Madison smiled and crossed to Lauren. "I didn't want to wake you. It seemed like you needed a few extra hours."

Lauren stepped into her lover's arms, her face burying itself against the warm curve of her neck, her arms wrapping around her waist. Madison held her tight, breathing in her scent. "Hello," Lauren whispered, feeling her body respond to her lover's closeness.

"Hello back."

"I'm just going to go find Megan," Alex told them. They never noticed her leaving.

"I was standing here hoping that I hadn't imagined it all...you being here. I was almost scared to go upstairs to check," Madison told her with a soft smile.

"Me, too. I woke up and I was suddenly so sad, thinking that I had dreamt it all again. Dreaming about you used to haunt me." Her mouth gently found the dark-haired woman's again. "Come back to bed, I'm not done with you yet."

Clarence stumbled to the door and was about to chew out whoever dared wake him at four in the morning, but stopped in mid-sentence when he saw Matt. He was still dressed in the same clothes as the night before and looked like he had not yet gone to bed.

"It's out."

"What is?" Clarence closed the door behind him as Matt charged in.

"Lauren's affair. It's out on the Grunge report. She got a call yesterday."

Clarence was suddenly alert. Damn, it was starting. "Where is she now?"

"She didn't say, probably the Cape. She always goes there when she is trying to get away."

"How many people know about that house?"

"I'm not sure. We've never talked about it to anyone."

"How the hell did it break? Who leaked it?" McLennan had too much to lose. After the debate Clarence had been very clear as to what information they held over his head. He would stake his career on the fact that the leak had come from someone else. McLennan's camp was not that stupid or self- destructive.

"Who the hell knows? Does it matter now? I want whoever leaked it to Grunge finished in this town, Clarence, is that clear?"

"First things first. We need to see if we can contain it. Does mainstream have it yet?"

Matt shrugged. "I haven't seen it in the morning edition yet." They sat for several minutes, lost in thought. This was it...the crash they had been expecting. The choice of responses was either counterattack or damage control; it all depended on what they had the stomach for. Matt sighed. "We need to get Lauren back here as soon as possible."

"She's not coming back, Matt. I think she made that clear."

"I think she will. She's still my wife. She is not going to hang me out to dry by myself." His conviction was born of years of knowing just how to manipulate her feelings and her weaknesses. He hadn't gotten where he was in politics without knowing exactly how to find his opponents' weaknesses and use that information to his advantage. Clarence looked at him, still skeptical, but said nothing else. "I have to get her back here to Washington."

Clarence turned. "Fine. I'll get the troops together. We need to focus on our response." This was it. The next few hours and days would determine the future of their campaign. Blow it and it was all over. But there was still a chance, *if* everyone played their roles perfectly. It was unnerving to also think that the outcome of the next forty-eight hours would depend to a certain extent on Lauren. And they needed to find her first.

Madison lay in bed suspended between sleep and full wakefulness. She savored the pleasant lethargy in her body that bespoke a long night and morning of lovemaking. Into that peacefulness, the scent of sandalwood drifted to tease her senses. *Lauren.* Her imprint was everywhere in this bed. Her scent clung to her skin, to the pillow beside her. She stretched with a slow smile as she came fully awake. *Maybe I should buy this bed from Alex and move it to my place,* she thought, her grin widening. She suddenly realized that Lauren was no longer sleeping beside her and decided to get up to look for her. She slipped on a T-shirt and loose baggy sweats and padded downstairs. As she went, she couldn't help the perma-grin stamped on her face. The grin disappeared of its own accord as she stepped into the kitchen and overheard Lauren talking.

"Matt, I'll see you tonight." Lauren flipped off her phone and turned, startled at a sound. She could not stop the quick flash of guilt that crossed her face.

Madison recognized it and stopped in the doorway, frozen. She felt panic rise. *Will Lauren be strong enough to stand firm against the pressure that is surely coming?*

"That was Matt," Lauren explained unnecessarily.

"Yes?"

"I have to go back tonight."

"Why?"

"He needs me. I have to go."

Madison looked at her quietly, feeling the numbness spread. *I need you,* she wanted to say; instead she stepped past Lauren to the coffee machine, needing to do something with her hands. "When are you leaving?" she finally asked.

Lauren pushed a hand through her hair, trying to read her lover's expression. "In a couple of hours. Are you angry?" *She doesn't look angry, she looks hurt.*

Madison paused as she was pouring herself a cup of coffee. "I'm not angry, Lauren. I'm trying to convince myself you won't back down when you get there, that you won't start doubting me and yourself, or worse, start weighing what you have to gain by staying with me against what you have to lose if you do."

"Honey, I don't know what else to do. I'm only going so that Matt and I can put up a united front as we formulate our response to the allegations. And try to do it without inflicting any further damage to his chances. I need to take care of this first, then I'll come back. Will you wait for me?"

Madison shook her head. "I don't know." Lauren looked at her, stunned. "I almost understand your reasons for going back. I can sympathize with them. I know you don't want his shot at the White House ruined, but every time you talk about it you keep forgetting an important piece. You. What *you* want. The point is you can't live your life to suit other people. The harder you try, the more restrictions they'll put on you just for the fun of seeing you jump through their hoops."

Lauren frowned, hurt that Madison could not accept her reasons for going. "It's not like that. My career is at stake here, too. I need to respond to this attack on my personal life. Me, not anyone else. Whether or not I come out is my decision and should not be left to some hack on the Internet. I can't leave it up to Matt's political team to come up with my response. It's my life, too."

Madison sighed. The joy of the last twenty-four hours was dissipated by the fear of going through the pain of losing her again. She looked at Lauren, torn between her love and her fears. Was she being unfair? Since she had arrived at Alex's the night before, her entire reaction to finding Lauren so unexpectedly there had been based on her feelings and emotions, and not on deliberating rationally about any of it. Lost in the wonder of being together again, they hadn't had time to talk and come to grips with what had happened between them years before. So much was left unsaid. Maybe she had just assumed too much. *We never have enough time*, she thought. She looked back at Lauren, her heart lurching with both fear and love.

"Do what you need to do, then. But, Lauren, sooner or later you're going to have to take a risk and trust what we have completely. Until you do, you're cheating me and you're cheating yourself. You can't outwit fate by standing on the sidelines and placing little side bets on the outcome of life. Either you wade in and risk everything to play the game, or you don't play at all, and if you don't play, you can't win."

Lauren felt the anger mix with hurt, the sharp little stab of it making her wince. Madison's words were hitting too close to home. She didn't want to examine her motives yet, afraid of the answers. "Is that what you think I'm doing?"

Madison stared at her for a beat. "I love you, Lauren, more than I have ever loved anyone in my whole life. I would do anything for you. You walk out that door, and my love will not stop because you are no longer here. But I am not going to wait for you to make up your mind about where you really want to be. Not this time. I can't live through that again. I once told you I didn't believe in ultimatums, well...I guess I lied. It's either him or me. You can't have us both. If going back is about you and your needs, then I will be here when you get back. If this becomes another battle to figure out how best to avoid making a painful decision, count me out. I'd rather feel the pain now." She turned to leave, and Lauren did not try and stop her.

As she walked into the terminal, Lauren saw Matt's driver standing to the left. She focused on placing one foot after the other as she headed toward the exit, the driver following closely on her heels. Holding herself together by sheer will, she did not want to think of anything else beyond getting home. She kept reliving the last hour in Boston, and the hurt on Madison's face when she told her she was leaving. She had wanted Madison to stop her, wanted her to beg her not to go. *But why? Because it was the coward's way out, that's why. The decision taken out of my hands, wasn't that what I was hoping for? So I wouldn't have to make it,* the annoying little voice inside of her head said. Maybe Madison was right. Maybe she kept placing little side bets, not fully engaging in her life so as not to risk losing. Her mouth tightened in annoyance. She hated it when the little voice was right. Safely sitting in the back seat of the car, she suddenly noticed that they were heading in the opposite direction from the house. "Ken? Where are we going?"

The driver glanced at her in the rearview mirror. "Sorry, Mrs. Taylor. I thought the senator had told you that I was to take you to a hotel. It seems the press is camped out in front of the residence."

She leaned back and closed her eyes with a sigh. *Great. That's just great.*

Madison returned home and, just inside the door, started to shed her clothing. Naked, she walked through to the bedroom, ignoring the blinking red light of her answering machine. She didn't care who was trying to reach her, or that somewhere on the Internet she was outed. The rawness of her feelings left her feeling even more exposed than some stupid story on the Web. She was past caring who knew that she was in love with a woman. And a married woman, to boot. *To hell with them all.* She slipped into a short navy blue robe, tying it loosely at the waist. Without worrying about the pieces of clothing she'd left lying here and there on the floor, she padded to the kitchen, took a glass from the cupboard, and grabbed a bottle of Scotch from the small pantry. She then went out to the back yard, leaving the patio door ajar behind her. She slumped down onto the deck chair, bare legs stretched out in front of her, and after pouring herself a shot, took a long swallow. She savored the heat of the alcohol as it warmed her throat, and fought off the sudden tears that threatened. *Damn it. Damn her again.* And damn her own weaknesses that kept her involved in the madness of loving someone when she should know better. She glared out into her yard, her fingers tightening on the glass, fighting off the urge to send it flying.

She had driven aimlessly around the city for hours, unable to make the decision to return home. She knew to the second the moment that Lauren had gotten on that plane. Up to that instant, she had hoped that Lauren would change her mind, or at least ask her to go with her. All irrational thoughts, but still... She heard the faint ringing of her doorbell and ignored it. *Go away,* she wanted to yell out; instead, she poured another shot, and this time forced herself to sip it slowly. *No sense in getting drunk too quickly.*

Her heart was breaking again, but this time it was different. As she sat there, she thought back over the previous twenty-four hours. *Would I want to wish the last day and night away? Would I want to take back being in Lauren's arms again? No.* That was the thing, wasn't it? She would not relinquish that glimpse of heaven, that chance to feel alive again, if only for a moment.

She sat quietly as she watched dusk fall. She'd always loved this part of the day when nature was suspended between daytime and nightfall. But tonight the lowering light only added a darkness to the yard to match her mood. She continued staring into the slowly deepening shadows, subconsciously registering that the ringing had stopped. Part of her heard the crunching noise to the side of the house, but it wasn't until she saw a pair of hands grab hold of the top of the fence that she realized someone was trying to climb into her yard. Before she had a chance to do anything, whoever was trying to scale her fence fell over the top with a clumsy thud followed by a curse. It was the curse that had her sitting back with a smile.

Darcy stood up, brushing the grass from her knees. "Fuck, I am getting old. I used to be able to do this drunk without falling down on my ass."

"You say fuck too much," Madison commented drolly.

"I wouldn't, if everybody cooperated." She stretched, feeling the bruising in her knee. "Bloody hell, didn't you hear me ringing at your door?" she asked as she went up the stairs, grimacing as her muscles protested this activity.

"Yeah."

"Why didn't you get the door?"

"I didn't know it was you. I didn't want to be bothered. I figured if it was someone I wanted to talk to, they would use their key. Why didn't you?"

"Why didn't I what?"

"Use your key."

Darcy stared at her, dumbfounded. "Fuck. I didn't even think of it." She left Madison smiling as she went into the kitchen and returned a few seconds later with a glass. She pulled over one of the other deck chairs and sat down, took the bottle from Madison's hand, and poured herself a generous shot. They sat in silence, quietly drinking as the steady hum of insects rose up all around them. The sweet smell of thyme drifted to them whenever the breeze danced through the herb garden.

"You okay?" Darcy finally asked.

"I guess. Why?"

"Lauren called on her way to the airport. She was worried about you."

"No need." Madison's jaw tightened, but she said nothing else.

"Want to talk?"

"No."

"Okay." Darcy took another sip and let the silence stretch between them. "Things will work out, Maddie."

"You think?" There was sarcasm at the edges of the word. Knowing she was being unfair to her friend, Madison waved her hand. "Sorry."

"She loves you."

Madison rubbed her eyes, the pain of that pronouncement squeezing her chest. "I know. Sometimes, though, when we are fighting past demons and a difficult history, love doesn't seem to be enough, does it?"

Darcy looked at her friend, at the wounded look in her eyes, and silently cursed Lauren for leaving. Just as quickly, she felt sorry for Lauren and what she was also going through.

Madison blinked and tried to clear the bright dancing spots

floating on her eyes. Then it happened again. The flashes left her
slightly disoriented. She sat in the car, unsure of what to do with
the press crowding around her in the faculty parking lot. It surprised her that they had found her so quickly. With a muffled
curse, she pushed the door open and reached into the back seat for
her briefcase as the questions rushed out at her.

"Dr. Williams, will you confirm that you were Lauren Taylor's lover?" "Do you know where Lauren is now, Madison?" The
questions were a constant barrage, the press and media unrelenting in their pursuit of what they perceived to be some hidden truth
in *the* scandal that would help break the monotony of their days.

"No comment," she mumbled. Another round of flashes went
off, forcing her to blink again to clear her vision. They pressed
closer, merciless in their hunger. In stunned fascination, Madison
registered that the smallest details of her past were being revealed
and reviewed in the shouted words assaulting her on all sides.

"Madison, how many married women have you been involved
with?" "How many times has Lauren Taylor called you? Your
phone records show calls from her recently."

That stopped Madison and she faltered, her startled eyes trying to find the person who had asked the question. "I said, and I
quote, 'no comment.'" Madison let the slamming of the car door
punctuate the sentiment. *My phone records? They're checking my
phone records?* She felt violated and lost. This time she blinked
off tears. She shoved her way through the crowd, her mind blocking out the questions, her heart aching for what she knew Lauren
would also face, was probably facing even now. *Oh, Lauren, I just
wished we could have made it without this circus*, she thought, as
she pushed her way into the building.

Inside her office, she half listened to the hundreds of messages on her machine. Everyone was looking for a comment. She
was almost amused as she heard the representatives from Larry
King and Barbara Walters asking for an exclusive. Her smile was
dry and without humor. *Go to hell, everyone,* she thought as she
erased them all. At the door there was a faint knock, and she
turned in time to see the pinched face of the department dean as
he entered. *He looks even more constipated than usual,* Madison
thought, swallowing the hysterical laugh that was hovering.

"Madison, do you have a moment?"

"Of course."

He stood just inside the door, looking like he was ready to

bolt at any moment. He stared past her right shoulder as he tried to find a way to start.

For a brief moment, Madison considered scaring him by moving into his line of vision, but decided that she was probably in enough trouble with the school so she stood waiting for him say his piece.

"We can't have this type of thing going on, Madison."

"What type of thing?"

"This...this is a serious institution of higher learning. There are people climbing up our trees and reporters going through our garbage!" He was almost purple in his outrage, his loose jowls shaking.

Madison tried not to laugh. This whole week was turning out like a bad movie. "I understand."

"I mean...please understand...it's not the rumor of your...of the... I mean, we don't have anything against...against it."

"It?" Madison asked, feeling a perverse satisfaction in watching him squirm in embarrassment.

He frowned at her over his half-moon glasses, the pinched look becoming even more pronounced. "We can't have classes interrupted and our student body distracted by this brouhaha, Madison."

"I agree, Dean. Perhaps I should take a short leave of absence until it dies down?"

"I was thinking that you should, I mean, the board was thinking that we could ask–" He stopped when her words registered. His smile was pleased, his relief evident. "Quite right. Splendid idea. Good, I'm glad that that's taken care of." Without another word, he left the office.

Madison sighed as she looked around. *Just like that, life changes on a dime.* She had no idea what her next step would be.

The air was thick with stale coffee and too many unfinished cigarettes left burning. Every inch of space in the hotel suite was used up. Piles of newspapers lay on every available surface, unwanted sections thrown carelessly on the carpeted floor. Heather sat at the wobbly desk, her laptop plugged in to the Internet. For over two hours she had been surfing for any mention of the affair, and if one was found she was downloading it to her hard drive. Some junior assistant—whose name Lauren had forgotten—was manning the phones. Someone had pulled the two television sets into a corner and left them flickering without sound on CNN and MSNBC. Every so often, another unnamed assistant flipped through the channels looking for headlines.

Lauren sat rigidly on one of the chairs, sipping from a bottle of water, bemused at the frenetic activity. It was almost on the same level as that of a campaign, but with more gloom. There was an ache in the pit of her stomach that she could not dislodge. When she let it, her mind kept drifting to the night she'd just spent with Madison, the remembered feel of her, the sweetness of being in her arms, the feeling that Madison was home for her. When that happened, she ruthlessly pulled her mind back to this hotel room and listened to the voices. She had glanced at the bold headlines, read the snippets of gossip during her flight back. Was she? Wasn't she? Would the senator comment?

There was more speculation than fact. That was the problem when reporters wrote a story based on rumors. A windbag of a columnist was now on CNN, discussing in knowing tones the impact that this revelation would have on the campaign.

"*Newsbeat* has it buried on page 13," a voice broke in.

Lauren sighed. *Thanks, Stephen,* she whispered in her head.

"The *New York Times* doesn't have it in the first section at all," another relieved voice chimed. And on and on it went, the play-by-play of "find the affair."

Lauren stood up and stretched, feeling her back muscles whimper a complaint. Her eyes found Matt who sat in a corner huddled with Clarence. *He looks like shit,* she idly thought. A flash of guilt followed. Unshaven, eyes bloodshot from lack of sleep, he looked more like a man possessed than a smooth politician.

Restless, wanting a break, Lauren started to move toward the door. Matt's icy blue eyes whipped to her. "Where are you going?"

"To get some air."

Unseen by Lauren, Matt motioned to his security chief, who stood up to casually lean back against the door, arms crossed in a pose smacking of nonchalance. Lauren froze, then she met Tom's eyes. He stared back at her impassively. Lauren's hands fisted at her side. "I'm a prisoner now?" she asked.

Matt ignored her question as he turned back to Clarence. She glanced around, desperate for an ally, but even Heather avoided her eyes. She turned to the window and crossed her arms, her hands cupping her elbows as a feeling of quiet desperation stole over her. *I wonder how Madison is doing?* And with that thought came the sweet ache of missing her, and the overwhelming urge to hear her voice. Instead, she toyed with the curtain and peered outside.

Madison collected all her papers and personal gifts and started to pile them into a second box. With that final pile came a sudden alarmed thought. How was she supposed to make a break for it carrying two boxes and her laptop? There was a soft knock at the door, but she ignored it.

The door opened slowly and a pert blonde peeked in. "Madison?"

Madison turned and recognized the woman. "Come on in."

Joan Landers, another professor in the department who had become a friend over the last several months, entered and stood hesitantly inside the small office. "I...I heard about what happened. I'm sorry."

Madison lifted a brow then quirked a forced smile. "Don't be."

"Is there anything I can do to help?"

"No, I think I've got it." She blew a breath, then turned. "Unless you can figure out a way of getting me out of here unnoticed."

After about an hour of waiting for Madison to reappear, most of the reporters were bored. Ambushing Lauren Taylor's lover earlier hadn't given them the sound bite needed, only a picture, so they continued to wait, leaning on their cars. Campus security had arrived and forced them off the main lot. Now the uniformed guards stood by the entrances, keeping a stern eye on them. Gary Whipper, a veteran of too many of these stakeouts, stood smoking lazily, trying to figure out a way of sneaking by security. His eyes narrowed against the smoke curling up from his mouth; out of the corner of his eye he saw movement on his right, over where he knew the service entrance was. He very casually flicked off his cigarette and, pretending that he was stretching his legs, inched closer to the driveway. The security guard, equally bored and looking into the distance, missed his move.

A petite blond woman wearing a white lab coat had gone back into the building and now was back, pushing a gurney out of the door. A white sheet covered what looked by the form to be a body, and the reporter slowed his step, a look of distaste on his face. A man got out of a waiting hearse and helped the blonde slide the stretcher and its repugnant cargo into the back of the car. The reporter had heard that the medical students practiced on cadavers, but just picturing what they might have done to the body had his breakfast jumping in his stomach. He watched as the blonde re-entered the building, then he turned back to the parking lot. *How long does the broad teach, anyway?* he thought grumpily. Inside the hearse, the driver turned the vehicle and pulled away from the entrance.

Gregory Niles had been awakened that morning at what was, to him, the ungodly hour of eight a.m. His girlfriend needed a favor, and if it had been anyone but her he would have hung up. Still, here he was, driving the borrowed transport, having gotten up despite only two hours of sleep, unshaven and bleary eyed, his thick blond hair sticking out in all directions in a very comical rendition of bedhead. *The sex she promised won't be enough,* he thought grumpily. *I'm going to ask for a steak.* He thought with glee about the look of horror that would cross his vegetarian girlfriend's face. He grinned as he slowly drove past the waiting crowd of reporters. Suddenly feeling happy, he almost waved at them. This was like driving the getaway car in a movie. Almost. He picked up speed as he left the university grounds. About half a mile from the university, he tapped on the glass partition.

Madison pushed the thick white sheet off and took a deep breath.

"Well, that's a first," she said aloud, glancing around with a faint shudder. She didn't want to think about her mode of transportation. *My time will come soon enough,* she thought with a grimace. She felt the car come to a stop and waited for the doors to open. She hopped out and stretched, noticing that they were now parked in a quiet spot by the south entrance of a small park. She turned to her rescuer with a grin. "Thanks, Gregory, I owe you one. Tell Joan there is no rush in dropping off my stuff. Nothing in there that can't wait a couple of days."

"Will do, beautiful."

As she walked away, she debated whether or not to go directly home. The press would probably be there. *Maybe Alex could help clear a path...* Then she remembered she didn't have a cell phone on her. She would just have to take her chances that the coast would be clear.

After two days of debate and discussions, they had made little progress in coming up with a plan. Each suggestion had been dismissed or analyzed to death, each point picked apart until there was nothing left. The frustration Lauren was feeling was elevated to a fever pitch and she felt ready to explode. She was exhausted and worried about Madison, and wanted nothing more than to talk to her. She also knew that if she never saw the inside of a hotel room again, it would be too soon. Heather looked across at her and smiled in sympathy. Lauren returned the smile automatically.

"So far, it's contained." Heather turned to Matt. "We are lucky that they have started bombing again in the Middle East; that has bought us some time. But we will need to comment soon. We can't hide from this forever."

Matt stood and rubbed tiredly at the back of his neck. "Respond with a 'no comment.'"

"That's not good enough, Matt. A no comment is the same as an admission."

Lauren frowned. "So admit it already."

Matt threw her a look and turned to Heather. "What are your sources saying?"

"Most are surprised, and 9 out of 10 don't believe it."

Lauren snorted. "Well, there you go. If they don't believe it, then it must not be true."

Heather glanced at her with concern, recognizing the stress and frustration in her eyes. Matt frowned at her. "This is not helping, Lauren."

There it is again. That damn patronizing tone I hate, Lauren thought with annoyance. "Really? Well let me tell you what is not helping: all of you trying to pretend that this whole thing is a mistake and is not true. The truth is that we *have* separated and I *am* gay, and this whole sordid mess needs to be addressed by saying it to everyone else. Then they should all get over it and concentrate on something that matters. People are dying in the Middle East, for crying out loud. Who I sleep with should be unimportant in the scheme of things."

"Funny that," Matt stated calmly. "Who *my* wife sleeps with is important to me, don't you think?"

The tension rose, and everyone in the room tried not to look at the two of them. Lauren released a long breath. "Matt, be reasonable."

"Reasonable?" Matt smiled, but his smile held no warmth. "I've been nothing but reasonable."

Lauren looked at him and, unbidden, the image of Madison's face rose. What was she doing here? What more could be gained? What did she expect her presence here would change? She was in love with Madison, who happened to be a woman. She wasn't the first woman to be in love with another; wouldn't be the first celebrity to come out—or the last. Appearing at Matt's side would not change how she felt. The hypocrisy of what they were trying to do made her suddenly ashamed. The pain and the longing for Madison were overwhelming. *How many people get a second chance?* It was time to take a stand. To hell with the consequences. "Enough." She didn't realize that she had spoken out loud until Matt stepped toward her.

"Enough, what?"

"No holidays together. No weekend getaways. No business as usual for the happy couple." She dismissed the options that had been put forth over the last day. "This whole thing of trying to find a way to lie our way out is a mistake. It's over. I'm in love with a woman. Have been for years. We can't go on pretending that it is not happening, Matt. We just can't."

Matt looked into her eyes and saw something in the golden depths that worried him. "Give me a minute with Lauren, everyone." After a brief hesitation, the group stepped into the other suite, throwing worried glances their way. Matt and Lauren were left alone.

Lauren turned to him. "I'm sorry, Matt. I can't pretend anymore. I thought I owed it to you to try and help you for the damage this will cause your campaign, but you know what? I've done my part these last few years. I've been sitting in this hotel room for the last two days trying to come up with a convincing lie to hide who I am. The irony is that it's because of lies that we are in this mess. I can't pretend I'm someone I'm not just so you can gain votes." Her eyes filled. "I'm losing my mind, Matt. I'm sorry,

I just can't do this anymore. It's over."

Matt sat down. His hands hung loosely over his legs and he stared at them for a moment. His thumb rolled the plain gold wedding band on his finger around and around. He knew it was over. He had fought it off as long as he could, but looking into her eyes he knew—she was not coming back. "I know." Shoulders slumped, he suddenly looked defeated.

For a moment, Lauren thought she saw tears, and her heart broke for him. She sat down beside him. "If I could have changed anything, I would have tried to handle all of this better. I never, ever wanted to hurt you."

He leaned back against the couch closing his eyes against the inevitability of their breakup. His hand scrubbed at his eyes. "I know, Lauren." He took a deep breath, then slowly released it, sat up and gave her a faint smile. For the first time in their relationship, he looked uncertain. "So, what do we do now?"

Lauren was surprised and touched by this vulnerable side. She took his hand and held it loosely in hers. "You issue a statement that acknowledges our separation. I'll do my part in responding, so leave that to me. But don't sell yourself short, Matt. You will make a great president."

He looked at the woman who had been part of his life for all of his adult years, and realized that he had lost something greater than any chance at a higher office. "And you would have made a great first lady."

Keith read the fax with a grim smile. "*As has been reported in the media, my wife Lauren and I are involved in a separation which we both expect to be amicable. All details regarding our marriage and divorce are personal to the two of us, and I hope the media will respect our privacy. I do not intend to make any further comment about this matter.*" Keith crumpled the paper and threw it out. "It was never personal, Lauren." He said it aloud, as if to make it more convincing to himself, then strengthened his tie. He had an interview to give.

Lauren looked out at the crowd shoehorned into her office. Word of her announcement had spread quickly, as it always did, and everyone was eager for her first comment. They were all salivating at the prospect of getting the details of this latest scandal to cut through the monotony of reporting the same tired news. She blinked when someone turned on a spotlight, white dots appearing behind her eyelids. For a moment as she looked at the familiar faces she felt uncertain, unsure about the next moment. It was, she was sure, more nerve-wracking to confront something so personal in front of people she knew—former friends and colleagues—than in front of a bunch of strangers. What they thought of her still mattered. She considered that with irony as she fought against the panic, twisting her hands in her lap as her nervousness spread. *What the hell am I doing?*

Darcy rang the bell again. "Are you sure she is home?"

Alex nodded. "I just talked to her half an hour ago. She's gone into hiding."

"Williams! Open the damn door." Darcy yelled to the wood. She tried the doorknob again and found it locked, as it had been every time she had tried it over the last ten minutes. She looked up at the face of the house, trying to see if any windows were open.

"We could try climbing through a window."

Alex gave her a look. "I'm supposed to stop breaking and entering, not participate in it."

Darcy grinned. "Good point. Maybe she is in the back." They made their way down the shared driveway and stopped at the fence, which was too high for them to see over.

Alex sighed in frustration. "Williams!" she called out, still getting no response. "Now what?" Alex asked.

"We climb it."

"We what?"

"We climb it."

Alex looked at the fence, then back at Darcy. She shrugged. "Well, here goes nothing." With a groan, she heaved herself over the top and landed heavily on the other side. She lay face down on the grass, winded. Darcy followed, but her aim was off and she landed heavily on top of Alex, who swallowed a mouth full of grass and dirt in the process. "Ouch! Get off me, you big lug." Alex spat dirt out of her mouth. "Christ, how much do you weigh, Stretch?"

"Shut up. From where I'm sitting, I have the advantage, and I'm taller than you are. I could sit on you for days and you wouldn't be able to do anything about it." They stood up, grimacing.

"I'm getting too old for this shit," Darcy muttered. They looked up to meet Madison's amused eyes.

She had heard the commotion from her bedroom window and come out to investigate, watching their progress in silent mirth. An index finger rubbed her upper lip, trying to hide the grin. "You know, Stretch, if you are going to continue to climb fences to impress the ladies, your form needs a little work. Though it's very knight-rescuing-the-damselish."

"Very funny." Darcy rubbed at a spot on her knee.

"Do you have an aversion to using the front door? That's what most other people do."

"It was locked. Why don't you ever answer your bloody door?"

"Why don't you use your key?"

Alex's eyes narrowed at that and she turned to glare at Darcy. "What?"

"Fuck. I forgot." Darcy winced as Alex turned to her with a snarl.

"Remind me to kill you later."

"What are you guys doing here?" Madison asked.

For a moment they looked at each other, puzzled, then Alex slapped her forehead. "We have been trying to call you for an hour, and it keeps going into your machine."

"I didn't want to be pestered by those damn reporters. What's up?"

"Have you been watching CNN?"

"I don't watch television, you know that."

"Lauren is supposed to give a press conference."

"What?" There was a pause as she registered the news, then as one they all rushed to the living room.

"Where the hell is the remote?" For what seemed like several minutes, they searched in vain. By the time they were done, the room looked like a hurricane had torn through it. Darcy finally found the desired object under the cushions of the loveseat, brandishing it in triumph. As if being closer to the screen would make a difference, they rushed to the set and turned the television on to the news channel. They watched as Lauren blinked into the bright light.

Madison felt her heart lurch at the pale face of the woman she loved. *She looks beat,* she thought.

Lauren smiled into the cameras. "Must be a slow news day." Laughter criss-crossed the room. She cleared her throat nervously, and her smile disappeared. "News should be considered a public trust. It was, and perhaps still is, what gives networks their dignity and integrity. It deserves respect and, as reporters of the news, so do we. But we must earn this respect. As a journalist, I stand before you embarrassed by my profession. We used to stand for something, to report the news that's fit to print. What should have been a very painful situation and a private decision has instead become a public circus, all for the sake of ratings. No one deserves this, not my husband, nor Dr. Williams, nor myself. How unfortunate that the truth of who I am, arrived at after many painful years, wasn't left to be dealt with in privacy by the three people affected."

She looked out at the room. This was it. She took a deep breath, the weight of making her admission falling from her shoulders. "I will not apologize for falling in love with an incredible person who deserves better than to be subjected to the lowest of what the press represents, but in love I am." She paused as her eyes swept the room. "It happens to be with a woman. That is not earth shattering news that will change America if reported. We should be reporting that every day children are killed and become killers in the Middle East. Or we should continue to wonder why people get behind the wheel drunk. My husband and I have filed for a separation, and I hope that we can be left to handle the rest privately. I believe that the American people are more open-minded than some of you give them credit for. In fact, I am counting on it. Matthew Taylor is a good man who will make a great president. The country will be lucky to have him." She suddenly gave a heart-stopping smile. "Now if you will excuse me, I have a plane to catch."

"Holy shit!" Darcy turned to Madison wide-eyed. "She just declared her love on fucking CNN."

Madison stood frozen, unable to process anything further, unaware that she was crying.

"You gotta do something." Alex finally said, a look of wonder on her face. "I mean this...this is big!"

"Jesus...this is too much. You think she might call you?" Darcy turned.

"What?" Madison asked, her brain unable to generate any

thought that remotely made sense.

Darcy and Alex looked at each other. "What should she do? Maybe try to call her?"

Alex shook her head. "Or we should get you a flight to Washington."

"Yeah, but what if she is going to the Cape?" Darcy added.

"Good point. She should go there. You should go there," Alex agreed, turning to Madison.

When the phone rang, they froze as the machine picked it up after the first ring. "Madison, it's Lauren."

"Wait!" They all moved toward the phone, stumbling and bumping into each other in their haste, impeding their own progress. Madison was the first to get there and grabbed the receiver as she tripped over a chair. "Damn...Wait...I'm here, don't hang up." She turned the machine off and leaned weakly against the wall, her legs shaking, ignoring her two friends, who were standing almost on top of her.

"Hello."

"Hello back."

"Did you happen to catch CNN?" Lauren's voice was uncertain.

"Yeah." Madison smiled, tears spilling down her cheeks. "You don't believe in small measures, do you?"

"Nope. It takes me a while to do something, but when I do, well..."

"Lauren...I..."

"I'm catching the first flight back; will you see me?"

"What did she say?" Darcy whispered loudly, straining to hear.

"Shh. I can't hear." Alex shoved at Darcy as she leaned further into Madison.

"Stop pushing."

"Be quiet, you guys." Madison growled at her friends as she tried to hear what Lauren was saying.

"What did you say?" Lauren asked, confused.

Madison leaned her head back against the kitchen wall and closed her eyes, tuning out her friends. "Nothing, just our idiot friends hoping for a happy ending."

"Me, too." The words were said softly but they carried across the miles, and to Madison were as sweet as a caress.

Madison rubbed the wetness on her cheeks, her heart full.

"Honey, just hurry home." Home. Such a tiny word...that suddenly meant everything.

"Don't pick me up at the airport. I don't want to say hello to you in front of hundreds of people. Okay?"

"'Kay."

"And, Madison? I love you."

Madison smiled through her tears. "You do pick your moments."

Epilogue

One year later

"I, Matthew Alan Taylor, do solemnly swear that I will faithfully execute the office of the president of the United States..."

Lauren stood watching Matt's inauguration with a quiet smile. There was pride for Matt mixed with a strange sense of disbelief. But for a twist of fate, she would be first lady today, standing on that platform on this cold windy January morning, watching Matt take the oath of office. Instead, she was standing in her living room, watching it like millions of other Americans—on television. She smiled at the irony of the moment. Lauren could have gone to the inauguration, as Matt had invited her. But she knew that her notoriety would have detracted from his moment.

In fact, she had found it hard to resume working as a journalist after delivering her bombshell. Being more famous than the people you were trying to interview was intimidating to some, competition to others. After months of futility and facing the prospect of being unemployed for the first time in her life, Lauren knew that a change was necessary. She had joined the faculty at Boston University in another brilliant ironic twist, just as Madison was leaving it permanently to resume her private practice. Lauren was now teaching ethics in journalism and starting to enjoy the different pace. What she was not enjoying though, was the tabloids' inability to let the story die. But that battle would be for another day. She turned when she heard a sound behind her, felt the small jump in her stomach that looking at her lover always triggered.

Madison stood indecisively in the doorway, unsure of Lauren's mood. *Is she regretting walking away from it all? Turning her back on the power, the fame and recognition? How does she feel seeing her former husband become president? It must be really weird.*

Lauren smiled at her and held out her hand. "Hello."

"Hello back."

She muted the sound and pulled Madison into her arms, kissing her throat, and then her mouth gently nipped her jaw line, pulling a soft moan from the dark-haired woman, a sound she was certain she was addicted to.

"Any regrets?" Madison asked as her eyes caught the flickering images on the screen.

"Yeah. That you have too much clothing on."

"Seriously, honey. This is a day that you were expected to share."

"Expected, perhaps, but never wanted." Lauren pulled back and looked into the smoky eyes of her love. "My only regret is that it took this long to be with you. I love you, Dr. Williams, more than I ever thought was possible to love another person. You have ruined me for anyone else."

Their mouths met in a long, soft kiss, the passion banked for the moment. Her fingers touched Madison's mouth in wonder. To want someone so badly was surely a sickness. "I crave your mouth like one craves water. Why do you suppose that is, Doctor?" Her finger traced the full lips, feeling the softness under her fingertips. "So, where did you come from?"

Madison kissed the fingers resting against her mouth. "Fate, or else I was the booby prize in the box of Cracker Jacks. And if this is an addiction, then I don't ever want to get cured."

Lauren smiled at her, the sheer wonder of being with her overwhelming. "I'm very lucky, then."

"No, I'm the lucky one."

"Fuck, will you guys hurry up getting ready? I would like to get lucky myself this century." Darcy slammed out of the house in frustration.

Newlyweds. It was always impossible to get them out of the door in any kind of sensible time. She shouldn't have offered to drive them to the party. She smiled suddenly, thinking about the last few months. To see her closest friends so in love... Jesus, if she wasn't a sucker for a happy ending. Who would have thought?

Jessica Casavant is an award-winning recording engineer, who decided the night a fight broke out between two actors, that she had had enough. There is only so much of someone else's vision a woman should take. She now works in the television industry, as a Toronto based executive. She can be reached at cdjc@sympatico.ca.

Printed in the United States
1078600004B/184

9 781932 300079